5 Bullets

Buck Edwards

This book is dedicated to Randy Russell—
an authentic horseman,
hatted, spurred and mustachioed.
Let' er buck, Randy.

Chapter 1

BELLS WERE RINGING IN the village down the road. Boone Crowe heard them, but he didn't know the reason for their ringing. It wasn't Sunday, and it wasn't the Fourth of July. No war had ended that he knew of, so the sound of their tolling echoing off the low hills was a mystery. Ahead, on the dirt road, he saw a man walking hurriedly, as if summoned by the bells. When Boone caught up to him, he hailed the walker.

"What's the celebration?"

The man, fortyish and dressed in overalls, his bare feet kicking up a dust, answered over his shoulder. "Hanging. Ned Butler."

Boone Crowe soured on that declaration and reined in his Ghost Horse. He was close enough to the little hamlet to see townsfolk scurrying toward the main street, stirring up their own dust. Having hung up his marshal's badge a year ago, he was no longer required to witness such despair, whether deserving or not. He'd overseen more hangings than he cared to remember and had even hanged a wicked slayer of children some years back up in the bear grass country. He'd been filled with rage that day and had stood, whether right or wrong, as judge, jury, and executioner to the foul old man.

Besides the actual hanging, it was the demented pleasure of the crowd that disgusted him. Children were often hoisted upon the shoulders of their fathers so as to afford them a better view. And many women, in Sunday dress, made their way to the front of the crowd, depending on the evilness of the crime committed. So Boone Crowe sat his horse and watched the farmer trot down the road until he finally disappeared into the crowd.

Ned Butler, he thought. The name meant nothing to him. Crowe admitted he was out of the circle of information this past year. He'd not seen anything of Judge Schaffer since he retired, which was fine with him. But there once was a time when he knew most of the lawbreakers in the territory. The bad ones, anyway. But no Ned Butler. He pushed his hat back off his forehead

1

and pondered his next move. His horse no doubt would like a drink of water, and he could use one himself, but there was nothing in that two-bit town calling him. Not now.

It was still a half-day's ride to Bentley Junction, where he'd agreed to help with a wild mustang roundup. A week earlier Crowe had put his wife, Rose of Sharon, on the eastbound train out of Fort Tillman, to help her friend Yelena in childbirth in Springfield, Illinois. She'd likely be gone a month or more. After two days of wandering around his ranch like a lost calf and eating his own cooking, he left the chores to toothless Rufus Mead, his hired hand, and the ex-marshal saddled up the Ghost Horse and headed off to cure his monotony.

It was his protégé, Rud Lacrosse, now the territorial marshal for Wyoming, who told him about the mustang roundup.

"You look glum as an old skunk, Boone," Lacrosse had told him, over a beer at the Occidental Hotel's bar.

"Rose is gone back east."

"So you've said now. Twice, in fact."

"Got any outlaws you need killing?"

"Not at the present."

"No rustlers?"

"I'm sure I could find a few if I looked hard enough."

Boone Crowe sighed. He pulled a cigar out of his vest pocket, looked at it, and then put it back. "Maybe I'll ride down to Fort Laramie. I haven't seen my old comrade, Lance Tunneson, in a couple of years. If the Sioux haven't scalped his carcass yet."

"That's not likely. Sitting Bull's doing the Cody circuit now."

"I heard that. A regular celebrity."

"Say, speaking of Fort Laramie. Why don't you go down to Bentley Junction? Some of them old cusses like you are rounding up mustangs. Got a contract with the army. They could use an old cow-roper like you."

"I ain't much with a rope. I'd do better in a buffalo hunt."

The two men sat in silence for a spell, attempting to look wise. Finally Crowe said, "Are they really having a roundup?"

2

"I heard they were. Heck, your old comrade, Sergeant Tunneson, might even be in on it."

Crowe stroked his whiskers. "He oughta be retired by now. Well, a ride down there couldn't hurt none. I wouldn't mind seeing some new scenery."

Lacrosse looked at the ex-marshal. "Scenery there is about the same as here, Boone."

But Boone Crowe was already turning the idea over in his head.

Now, three days later, here he was, sitting on the Ghost Horse, watching from a distance a town gone mad with a lynching.

Sergeant—then Corporal—Lancelot Tunneson rode with Boone Crowe down into Mexico after the war, chasing reluctant Confederates bent on joining in the mischief of Mexican politics. After four long years of war, disillusioned and discontent, both men realized eventually that army life was all they were familiar with. Crowe, who had elevated from private to major in the conflict, gave up his commission for sergeant stripes, and led, along with Tunneson, a company of sharpshooters into the unbearable heat of the Mexican desert.

It became a year of skirmishing with the Apache and Comanche as well as defeated Rebels. One night, after a day of blistering one-hundred-degree swelter, the temperatures plummeted at night to an enigmatic, star-clustered agony of bitter cold. It was here that, as dawn approached, a hunting-turned-war party of Comanche came howling over the hill, putting a surprise fight to Crowe's company. Fighting Johnny Rebs was what most of this outfit was used to—fighting Indians was something altogether different.

By full light, the company had taken six killed and four more wounded. What wasn't taken from the troops in death took them in spirit. Having done their damage, the Comanche rode off with victorious whoops, and half of the company's horses. Crowe and

Tunneson stood in reproach of themselves for having not been more prepared. Walking the battle site, they counted eight dead Indians. "We'll call it even," Crowe said. "But let this be a lesson to us, Lance. This is not Shiloh or Chickamauga. Even Cold Harbor was different from this."

In the years that followed, Crowe and Tunneson fought side by side, each receiving wounds, both from arrows and from bullets, each man aiding the other. But once the wayward Rebs were brought to heel, the two fighters were transferred north, to where the Sioux and Cheyenne stirred up their own mischief. New names became household words—Crazy Horse, Sitting Bull, Gall, and others—carrying with them no small degree of terror. Both men missed the fight on the Little Bighorn River, having come days later to witness the bleached bones of Custer's 7th Cavalry. Consigned to burial duty, Crowe and Tunneson began to see the reality of the situation, and knew—working through the stench of death, so akin to the slaughter they had already witnessed in Virginia in the last days—that war, in any form, was the lowest of contributions to mankind.

One year later, when the US Army began moving against Chief Joseph and the Nez Perce, Boone Crowe left his position as scout. Here was his line in the sand. The Nez Perce had always been his friends. "I got no bone to pick with them," he told General Howard. And so his army days came to a close. Tunneson remained, but once the tribe had surrendered, he was so moved that he later presented his saber to Joseph as a token of apology. He felt that taking part in the Nez Perce War was the biggest black mark on his military career.

It was nearing dark when Boone Crowe rode onto the grounds of Fort Laramie. The old ramparts had long ago been removed and now took on more the appearance of a trading post than a military facility. There were the infantry barracks, the officers'

4

quarters, appropriately named Bedlam, and the parade grounds with an occasional cannon, with the American flag snapping in the wind, but there was also an array of Indian dwellings scattered about, from tipis to wickiups.

"Can I do something for you, mister?" It was a private, holding the reins of a horse near the open door of a clapboard building.

"I'm looking for Sergeant Lance Tunneson. Is he about?"

The horse holder, no more than a boy, shook his head. He looked up at the old marshal and said, "No, he's not about. Been gone somewhere for three days now."

Crowe scratched his whiskers. "Who's in charge here, private?"

"Well, it would be Colonel Beach, but he's plum gone too. Not certain, but I heard Denver. Some army business."

"Who's left then?"

The soldier nodded his head in the direction of the open door, where a string of voices could be heard. "Captain Gillespie."

Crowe tilted his hat off his brow and bent an ear toward the voices, but it was nothing but a series of echoes. Finally, after a minute, a lone soldier tramped out of the building, his face a flush of anger. He strode past Boone Crowe and the private without a look or a word. Directly behind him came a tall, dark man, holding a riding crop in his hand, slapping its feathered-leather end against his boots. For a moment he watched the retreating figure crossing the parade ground, a smile of satisfaction on his face. Finally he looked at the private.

"Did you water this beast?"

"I did, sir. But..." The young soldier lifted his face in the direction of Boone Crowe, who was still sitting on his horse.

The captain frowned. "But what?"

"This here fella was asking for Top Sergeant, sir."

"He ain't here."

"I told him that, so he was asking fer you, sir."

Captain Gillespie lifted his gaze reluctantly in the direction of

Crowe. What he saw was a grizzled old saddle tramp, covered with the dust of the trail.

"He's looking for Sarge," the private went on.

"You said that already, soldier. Maybe this fellow has a tongue of his own. Unfortunately I'm too busy for chit-chat."

In the short span of a minute, Crowe had come to the easy conclusion that this officer was a horse's ass. He'd seen a hundred of them over the years, from army officers to fresh lawmen and bounty hunters to haughty women. He had no tolerance for any of their kind. But he wanted some answers, so he'd try and endure this puffed-up captain long enough to get a bit of information.

With a display of his own showiness, Crowe slowly dismounted from the Ghost Horse, and stepping to the private, took the reins of the captain's horse from him. He put his gloved hand to the horse's ear and rubbed it affectionately. Then he put his hand on the private's shoulder and nodded. Both a little confused yet pleased, the young man stepped back.

"Here's what I think," Boone Crowe said. "Whatever answers I need will take but a minute. Maybe two. So, either I get those two minutes here, or I ride alongside you until you tell me what I need to know. Pretty simple."

Captain Gillespie felt the sting but had the sense to keep quiet. "Who might I be addressing," he said.

"Name's Crowe. Boone Crowe. Retired United States Marshal for Wyoming Territory. I served at this fort as a scout before marshaling. Lance and me go back a long ways." He wasn't in the mood for any snobbery from the captain, official or otherwise, so he added, "We go back to before you were born, most likely."

The captain's mouth came open then closed again. Finally he said, "I have a lot of pressing business to attend to, Mr. Crowe. I understand your concern for Sergeant Tunneson, however—"

"No, you don't. I rode a long way to get here. And I'm not in the mood for so-called pressing business. So let's dispense with the pleasantries and find a place we can talk. If that suits you?"

The captain's face flushed with anger, but he reluctantly jerked his thumb toward the open door. Inside, Gillespie motioned to a hardback chair while he sat on the edge of his desk, feigning impatience. Another soldier, a corporal, sat at another desk. "Fetch us some coffee, will you Higgins," he commanded. The corporal disappeared without a word into an adjoining room but returned in less than a minute with two tin cups and a pot of coffee.

"It's still hot," he said, handing out cups.

Crowe removed his hat, took the offered coffee, and drank its bitter blackness.

Gillespie did likewise, then sat behind his desk. "I won't find another man like Sergeant Tunneson. Not if I searched the whole territory. That's why I sent him out with a small troop."

Boone agreed with a nod. "Sent where?"

The captain shifted uncomfortably in his chair. "You might have noticed those civilians camped out in the brush. They were wranglers hiring on for a roundup of mustangs. The army can't have enough mounts. And since the red men have been tamed, we don't have the problem of horse thievery we once had. Still—"

"Get to the point, captain," Crowe said.

Gillespie tried not to show his irritation at this interruption. After a pause, he said, "I sent Tunneson out on the trail of some deserters. He had that Straw Dog with him. Claims that Indian rode with him since Custer's blunder."

Crowe took another drink of the bitter coffee. "Deserters?"

"We've had a rash of them lately. Usually they slip away, one at a time. Sneaking into the night like scared pups. But...well, the bunch Tunneson is after numbers six. We might have just let them be, as we're better off without them. But words come down to us that they are a bad lot. A very bad lot. And they've been terrorizing some of the settlers."

"I'm listening," Crowe said.

"I sent the sergeant out with four more men. Three days ago. Early this morning Straw Dog rode in with word that they had made contact with the deserters."

"What does contact mean?"

"Well, according to the Indian, the deserters were well-armed and holed up in a canyon somewhere. That's the story, anyway."

"Are you doubting Straw Dog's word?"

"It's a wild country, marshal. Without any witnesses, it's hard to say what's happening."

Boone Crowe looked into his coffee mug, examining the dredges. Gillespie had his witness; he was simply too much of an Indian-hater to realize it. Or to believe it. He stood up and thanked the corporal for the coffee. "Do you mind if I poke around for a while, captain? I've had a hard ride."

"Were you planning on joining the roundup, marshal?"

"No," Crowe said sharply. "I was down here to see my friend. I'll be moving on in the morning."

"Well, you're welcome to sup with the men tonight, if your pallet can handle army chow."

The old marshal put his hat back on and left without another word.

There were campfires burning inside the fort's perimeter. After tending to the Ghost Horse, Crowe strolled the grounds looking for Straw Dog. Every soldier he encountered pointed in a different direction, claiming to have seen the scout here, and then there. Finally, one trooper, bent over his boots with bootblack and a piece of cloth, invited the old lawman to join him in a swallow from his jug. "Ain't seen Straw Dog since you rode in. But I know where he is."

"Where's that?" Crowe asked, having, out of curtesy, taken a drink from the whisky jug.

"Back from where he came. Wherever the Sarge is. I was in the listening vicinity of his conversation with Gillespie. Straw Dog said Sergeant Tunneson sent him back for some reinforcements and an ambulance. Told the captain there was a standoff."

"And what did Gillespie say."

The soldier tipped up the jug and took a long drink. "Aahh," he said. "That'll do."

Crowe waited.

"Captain told Straw Dog that Tunneson would have to work out his own problems. He said he had his own to deal with." The man wiped his mouth with his sleeve. "So, I never actually seen Straw Dog leave, but his horse is gone. He's like a ghost anyway, you know."

Boone Crowe's face turned pale with rage. "Where? Where are they?"

"That wise old redskin laid it out plain as a spellin lesson. But by then the captain was already walking away. But I heard Straw Dog say it was two days ride, maybe less. West. Antelope Hills, he said. Wherever that is."

Crowe took another swig from the offered jug. "I know where it is." Fishing in his vest pocket he found two cigars. Handing them both to the soldier, he said, "Much obliged." Then he stood.

"Where you headed, mister?"

Crowe looked into the dark night, watching for a moment the dancing flames of the campfires. "Antelope Hills," he said.

Chapter 2

THE SIX RIDERS RODE upon slow, worn out Army mounts, lather dripping from their nostrils, the heavy wheezing gasps of exhaustion like the chuffing of failing engines. Cletus Burke raised his hand in the air, indicating a halt. As he turned, looking over his shoulder at the riders behind him, he saw the first horse collapse, falling to its knees, then hard over on the ground, legs moving like slow pistons in the empty air. The man on his back, Pup Murphy, managed to jump free of the saddle but ended up falling facedown himself in a puff of dust.

Everybody watched as Murphy stood, brushing himself off. No one spoke. They, like their horses, were too done-in to waste energy on words. Cletus Burke nodded at Pup Murphy and so the soldier pulled his army-issue Colt from his holster and moving close to his struggling horse, put a bullet in the animal's head. The sound of the shot startled the other horses and they erupted into a fatigued dance, kicking up more dust.

"Alright. Git down," Burke finally commanded.

He watched as the rest of the band dismounted. They were still in army uniforms, though they had quit the army three days prior, following a plan they had concocted in the barracks tent that they shared. They were a like-breed, each coming from the backstreets of New York City where violence between gang factions was a way of life, if not always of survival. Most of their fathers, brothers, or uncles had been part of the clenched-jaw ferocity of animals stalking the alleyways during the height of political tensions in the city's Five Corners during the Civil War. They had resisted inscription, vowing to fight and die in the streets rather than be killed in some faraway cotton field, in a war they could care less about.

But this group of underlings, the offspring of a rebellious era, eventually felt the heat of their own street crimes, and so, one by one, they fled the city and took up their chances with the Army of the West, where a different kind of criminal passion awaited them. Cletus Burke, self-appointed leader, ruled mostly in his own fanciful mind. This was not a band to be managed and each of the others waited his chance to break out on his own. But because Burke had been in Wyoming Territory longest, and had been on enough patrols to know better the country, the others acted as temporary followers.

"I thought you said we'd see some Injuns." This from Baby Sullivan, who was the youngest of the group. He owed the moniker to his small stature and a youthful face full of freckles that masked an unchecked viciousness. "And I don't mean them drunken ones hangin round the fort."

Finn O'Clery, who was the oldest, a leftover from the actual gangs of New York City, a white bearded, scorpion-faced fighter who had done battle with hatchet, sword, and pistol in the early days of Tammany politics and had the marks to attest to it. Leathery-skinned with one eye creased by the crooked white scar of a twenty-year-old knife fight. O'Clery feared nothing. "You'll find most Injuns is plum tamed-up, Baby. You'd be better off makin war on the whores in Cheyenne." He laughed hoarsely.

"The plan's the same," Burke said. "Peacock's tradin post ain't that far. That's where we'll get fresh horses. And we can get shed of these army rags too. After that, I don't give a damn where you go or what you do."

"What about that patrol doggin us?" Baby said.

O'Clery laughed sardonically. "We cut them boys down by three back in the canyon. Tunneson's half strength now. He's likely licking his wounds."

"Well, by-cracky, if he wants another fight, we'll give it to him," Baby Sullivan said.

"My bet is he's limpin back to the fort," Burke said.

Two men stood off to the side, neither speaking. Will Byrnes was young and was already feeling the blunder for having joined this party. The other man, L. P. Quinn, was an island. He spoke little and listened a lot. He, more than any of the others, was itching to get away, not just from the army, but from this star-

12

crossed band of misfit deserters. But L. P. Quinn also knew the value of patience. So he would wait, scratching his red beard and attending to his own business.

"What about this tradin post?" O'Clery asked.

"I ain't certain, but I think it's on the far side of that crest there. Run by old man Peacock. He's married to a transplanted Cheyenne woman from Nebraska, or some damn thing. On patrol we watered our horses there aplenty." He rubbed his forehead with the back of his hand. "I seen a few blanket Injuns hangin bout the place some days too."

Baby Sullivan was getting excited now.

"And horses. Last time I was there, they had a pole corral with some runners penned up."

"You want I should go do some killin?"

"Shuddup, you damn fool kid. We're there for horses and outfits, not blood."

"Not blood," the kid fumed. "What about those blue boys we ambushed back yonder? Ain't that—"

"Go rub down yer horse, Sullivan," Burke burst. "You'll be ridin double. Pup's horseless now, so you'll carry him."

"Why me?"

"Because I said so. I'm tired of yer uneducated mouth." Burke spit on the ground. "Ain't no reason to hurry now. So rest up them horses. We'll leave in the morning. First light."

O'Clery stepped up alongside and put his hand on the kid's shoulder. "Yer teasin the tiger, boy. Best do as yer told."

Baby Sullivan stared up into Burke's face, but the leader turned away.

Sergeant Lancelot Tunneson had not turned back to the fort. The ambush in the canyon had not been his blunder. He had left the half dozen men under Corporal Coleman's watch, with instructions to skirt the canyon while he and Straw Dog scouted ahead. But Coleman, like so many anxious young soldiers, misinterpreting the order, found himself trapped under a fuselage of bullets, killing three, including Coleman himself.

Hearing the gunfire, Tunneson put his Sharpes into long range action, sending Burke's deserters on the run again. But the damage was done. He sent Straw Dog back to the fort for help, then spent the rest of the day wrapping the dead in tent cloth and securing them to their mounts.

"This is not a pleasant thing," Tunneson said, "putting your comrades in the ground like this. And all for a foolhardy mission." He removed his kepi and swiped his bandana across his forehead. "Be thoughtful, men. And think hard on the bastards that done this. You used to eat yer chow next to them. Pulled guard duty and played cards. But they are no longer your comrades. They are your enemy now."

Their solemn task completed, the remaining troopers stood before their sergeant with sober faces. Most of them had missed the battles with the Indians, instead biding their time performing meaningless duty patrolling the plains under a hot sun or drifting snow, watching over a people already conquered. For many of them, this was their first encounter with flying bullets and sudden death, and it showed on their faces.

"These are stupid men. I know where they're going," Tunneson said. "Some of you have been there yerself…with me."

"Peacock's?" uttered a private.

Tunneson nodded. He looked hard at the young men before him, and then at the shrouded bodies draped over their horses. "This was Captain Gillespie's affair. But as far as I'm concerned, it's over. Private Cohen, I want you to take this party back to the fort. If Gillespie wants to know what happened, then I'll give a full report on my return. I'm too old to bury more boys for the likes of this trash. At least with the Indians we had a respectable foe."

"What are you goin to do, Sarge?" Cohen asked. "You can't go this alone."

"I'm not," he lied. "I'll just do some trackin for a spell. See if my hunch was right…about Peacock's. Straw Dog should be here in a day or two with reinforcements. Now get mounted up and skedaddle. You got two days ahead of ya."

The men mounted, and leading their burdens, moved off eastward, toward Fort Laramie. Sergeant Lancelot Tunneson watched them go for a long time, until their blue backs mingled with the tall grass and red sun of the afternoon.

Amadeus Peacock stood facing the westward dying sun, as was his evening ritual these past dozen years. He walked across the yard, from his porch to the pole corrals, where a colorful throng of horseflesh was milling about. In another week he would be selling these to the army, the finale to a three month's effort in gathering this stock. His riders, Bull Head and the half-breed, Henry Mussel, had combed the saw grass of the upper Wind River for this herd, and the strong heads and long legs of these spring mustangs spoke for themselves. The two riders had been hard at breaking them to a saddle, but now the job was done.

Turning back to the log structure that served as the trading post, Peacock smiled at the light that was visible in the east window. It was good to have the girl, Iron Hand home again this past year. She'd been a help in the store, and with his wife, Sarah Bird, and the Turtle woman, whose notorious steadiness in trudging through her daily chores, was fitting of her tenacity and her name. Even though the girl returned from the white man's Indian school with a heart full of anger, she had managed to temper it some, thanks to the silent attentions of Henry Mussel.

Colonel Beach had promised to send a squad of soldiers to collect the animals and write a receipt for payment. It would be soon, he was sure. In the meantime, it was good to watch the horses on these twilight visits. His own riding days were long over, thanks to an arrowhead that lodged itself in his knee fifteen years past, down on the Brazos in Texas. He had fled that wild country of Comanche and Apache, and rescuing the captive Turtle from a starving winter a year later, he had settled with the Shoshone and opened up shop. His supply wagons came in by rail on uneven schedules, and so he made due with collecting horses for the army between shipments of wares.

The old man limped back to the store, and in the dim light he found his wife, Sarah, bent over a half barrel of soapy water. When she looked up at him, he did not see an old woman, rather the prettiness of her youth, a prettiness that had been passed on to her niece, the girl, Iron Hand. He scolded her for working late, and when she raised herself up, he seized her and put a kiss on her forehead.

She shook him off, hiding her smile. "Fool," she said.

Lancelot Tunneson lay in his bedroll with a foreboding unease. After sending off his column of soldiers, living and dead, he had ridden to a place where he could watch the trail leading to the trading post. It was his intent to ride all the way, but he'd pushed his horse hard, and if he rested now and rose early, he could still get to Peacock's in time to give a warning. And his warning would be this—give the bastards whatever they want. Knowing the deserters had killed half of his troop, their bloody desperation was clear.

He thought about his young Claire, whom he'd lost so many years ago. On this strange night it was as if she was still near. Camped, as he was, beneath a cluster of elms, he'd made a small fire for coffee but had no appetite for food. Even the coffee was more ritual than desire. He had many regrets, and they came back to him in force here under the shadows off the trees. He had shown courage a thousand different times in a thousand different ways, but three days ago his courage had buckled. For months he had pondered it, and for weeks he had settled on it, to the point of acting upon it. The very day that Captain Gillespie came to him and ordered him to strike out after the deserters, he had already penned his resignation.

But returning to his quarters, and staring down at the ink scratches on the paper, his courage faltered and he threw the paper in the fire. Only God in heaven could know what might have happened had he laid that paper on Gillespie's desk. Might those men of his squad, led by someone else, still be alive? He was a soldier. He knew better than to question his judgements, but that's what he was doing now. He should have followed his friend Boone Crowe out of the army back in the seventies. *What the hell had been the point in staying?* he wondered.

But he had stayed. And it was the face of another woman that had kept him close. Tunneson heard a noise in the treetops and he stood, moving away from his fire. The night was unearthly dark now, and he stood for a long moment, trying to gauge the source of the sound. Then it came, the low, hollow hoot of an owl. It was speaking to him. And suddenly, as if applying its own ambush, the owl dove from the tree branches and, swooping down with flapping wings, passed mere inches over Tunneson's head, another hoot trailing off behind.

A shiver, cold as a snake, slithered down the sergeant's back. He knew what that meant.

The owl had called his name.

Chapter 3

THE GHOST HORSE COULD feel the tension in its rider's legs, and the pounding of his breath as he leaned forward in the saddle. But Boone Crowe was not a fool, and even driven now by an anxious purpose, he was not about to ride his beloved pale horse into the ground. Fort Laramie was behind him now by a full day, and as stealthy as Straw Dog was, it had been easy for Crowe to pick up the Indian scout's trail. He had already chewed off the end of an unlit cigar, and his stomach gave a chorus of bear-like growls from hunger, but he kept on, tacking up the miles.

Crowe had practically nothing to go on, only the general notion of trouble, based on secondhand information from the jug-tipping trooper at the fort. But Straw Dog's overheard conversation with the captain had all the makings of truth. Crowe himself had not been impressed with the vainglory impetus that seemed to drive the young officer. But to refuse even a second thought in regard to Tunneson's safety, and request for help, stretched beyond the pale of military decency, much less protocol.

After the debacle in the southwest with the Comanche raid, Tunneson vowed he'd never again put his men into needless danger. He went so far as to make Boone Crowe promise to hold him to his word. No more carelessness. *I have to forget about the war, Boone, and train my mind for plains fighting. It ain't the same out here.* But the stench of the dead at Little Bighorn was a smell that had never left their nostrils, and it was not difficult to see the change that came over Tunneson. In hindsight, Crowe wondered if his friend might have become too cautious, which created an entirely different kind of danger.

It was in this haze of thoughts that the ex-marshal saw the bedraggled line of soldiers coming toward him through a grassy draw—three mounted troopers leading three horses burdened with the dead. Crowe dismounted and waited for their approach. The lead soldier lifted his hat in Boone's direction, and finally dismounting himself, came forward.

"Are you from the fort? I'm Private Cohen, sir."

Crowe recognized the familiar mix of weariness and distress in the young man's eyes and had not forgotten the many times he too had worn that same look. And now, studying the canvas-wrapped bodies, he felt a similar chocking rise in his throat. A heat, that had nothing to do with the hot sun, spread across his neck and face. *How many ways to die in this country*, he thought. Finally, gathering himself, he said, "Name's Boone Crowe, son."

Cohen seemed to straighten up. "I've heard of you. From Sergeant Tunneson. He—"

"Is...is Tunneson among these?" He pointed to the dead.

"No, sir. It was him who sent us back. He said..." The private's voice trailed off.

"He said what?"

"Well, Mr. Crowe, the sergeant took this thing pretty hard. He blamed himself."

"Where is he, then?"

Private Cohen swallowed, his eyes searching the surrounding country for the words. "I know you musta been his friend. At least he said you was. And I rode with Sergeant Tunneson myself for near a year now. But...well, he seemed different. He was saying things that didn't sound like the old sarge."

"Like what?"

"He said...he said, 'This is the end of it.' He said that a couple of times. And then he asked me if I had a gal somewhere. Like, back home. Why, he plum knows I don't."

"Does he have anybody with him?"

"No, sir. That too. He said he was going to follow this bunch to the end. But...there's six of them and only one of him. Oh, and the Indian. Straw Dog."

"You met Straw Dog on the trail too?"

"Yes, sir. Half a day back. He was mighty upset. He said some funny things too. Not funny, just strange coming from him."

"Like what?"

Cohen took a long look into the flat grassland. "I don't know how he meant it, Mr. Crowe. And I don't know if it was just Indian talk, or what. But he said when he was done with these deserters, he was…he was going back and kill the captain. He said he wouldn't rest till Gillespie…" The private blinked nervously.

Crowe waited. "Go on, son."

"He said he wouldn't rest until Gillespie's scalp was hanging from his belt."

Crowe's memory went back to Gillespie and the image of the captain's curly black tresses that hung Custer-style down the back of his neck.

"Where'd Tunneson say he was going?"

"He figured Burke was leading them to Peacock's place. That tradin post back yonder. He figured they'd be wanting horses. And they'd be itching to get loose of their uniforms."

"And he was fixin to face them alone."

"It appeared that way. I tried a couple of times to talk him out of it. But he just said he wanted to check things out. Didn't really say nuthin about having a showdown. Like I said, he was acting different."

"You said Burke. Is that one of the deserters?"

"Yes, sir. Six all total."

"Who are the others? You got names?"

"They aren't writ down anywhere, but I know 'em all. I can tell you their names."

"I need them on paper. Six is too many to remember."

The private queried the other soldiers, and after a few minutes the stub of a pencil was produced. Cohen himself took a much-read letter from his side pocket and, removing the two pages of correspondence, took up the envelope and scratched out the names. After some time, the names were handed to Crowe, and he looked at them with the concentration of a former lawman. "Who's this Baby Sullivan? Is that his real name?"

"Never heard a different one. That's what everybody calls him. He's crazy, Mr. Crowe. Plum crazy."

Crowe looked at the names again, then back to Cohen. "We

both got places to go." He reached for the reins and, patting the Ghost Horse on the neck, put his boot in the stirrup and swung into the saddle.

"I didn't want to leave him, Mr. Crowe. I really didn't. But he ordered me."

Boone Crowe liked this young man. If soldiering was what he ended up doing for a spell, he'd be a good one. "Man reaches a certain age, Cohen, when his past starts catching up to him. It's like a shadow, son. Pretty soon it starts getting so close yer not sure which is the shadow and which is you. And the next thing you know, the shadow's speakin for you."

The private nodded solemnly.

"Carry on, Private Cohen," Crowe said, and he gave the young soldier a crisp salute.

Ain't no way I'm packin that damn Pup Murphy on my horse.

Baby Sullivan let these thoughts stoke an inner fire in him, which fueled his rage at Cletus Burke, and then one by one, to all of the others. What was left of the day had worn on into evening, and Sullivan began making quiet preparations for what he considered his early escape from this pack. If there was Indians down at that trading post, he was going to get himself some. The big long war with the red man might be over for the army, but it wasn't over for him. Not yet. Baby Sullivan was going to leave his mark.

Seemingly undetected, he moved his horse closer to the edge of the camp, distancing himself from the others. And once darkness was complete, he moved stealthily to where Will Byrnes was sleeping, and pilfered some extra cartridges from the other's saddle pouch. Byrnes army issue revolver was lying holstered, nearby, and the temptation was too strong, so Sullivan snatched it up too.

Back in his bedroll, Baby lay awake, listening to the snores of the others, waiting for the hour when he'd creep away. According to Burke, the trading post was less than an hour's ride, due west. His horse probably would take him there on its own, especially if it smelled water, or other horses. This was what his Pa used to call, a waltz in the park.

Hours passed. Sullivan watched the moon reach its zenith and then beyond. The fire was nothing but a fading red glow. Rolling out of his blankets he crawled on hands and knees until he reached a place away from the camp where he could stand. With quiet care he placed the saddle on his mount and chinsed it up, the horse showing no resistance. A voice from the camp stopped him.

"What are you doing?" It was Burke.

"I'm just relievin myself, dammit." Baby waited a long time for a reply but none came. So he took the horse by the reins and led it down through the draw and onto the flat. He gave one last look at the moon, then put his boot in the stirrup and mounted. He looked to where he believed west was, and, giving heel to his horse, rode away.

Back in the camp Burke was standing. Baby Sullivan was an open book, and he'd watched the kid through all of his preparations. "Git up," he roared. "It's time to ride. Sullivan's broke off. Fixin to git us all killed. Damn kid."

"Why didn't you shoot the little bastard?" Finn O'Clery bellowed, crawling from his bedroll?

"Hell. Now I'm afoot," Pup Murphy cried.

L. P. Quinn said nothing, simply moved to the horses. He didn't like any of these men and the sooner he could get away from them, the better. But he needed the same thing they did—new clothes and a fresh horse. What Burke didn't know was that Quinn too had been to Peacock's little store, once with Tunneson. On that day he had sat on his horse while Tunneson parlayed with the old storekeeper. Then, from inside the store came three women, all Indians. One was an old squaw, Peacock's wife. Another one was young, about twenty. Quinn had stared at her for a long time. Black hair with deep angry eyes. *A looker*, he thought, *for an Indian*. But when she returned his stare, it was filled with hate.

The third woman was between the two, maybe in her thirties. Handsome features. But what surprised Quinn was how Tunneson acted when he saw her. He went straight to her and the two of them spoke words, soft, tender words, it appeared. They both smiled and at one point the woman put her hand on Tunneson's shoulder. It seemed more than just a friendly gesture. It was something more, and Quinn licked his lips. *Here's a tale*, he thought.

So, as the troop of deserters set out after Baby Sullivan, Pup Murphy now riding double with Will Byrne, L. P. Quinn knew what else he wanted when they got to Peacock's.

In the first dim light that shot across the waves of Wyoming grassland from the east, Sergeant Tunneson saw a lone rider galloping hard down the trail from the rim rocks. One, not six. *Who is it?* he wondered. *Straw Dog?* From this distance, in the dim light, it was impossible to tell, but it was obvious horse and rider were heading the same place he was—Peacock's store. Putting spurs to his own horse, he raced to cut off the rider.

Baby Sullivan, absorbed in his blood lust, did not see the approaching rider until he was almost upon him, and then all things became clear. It was the damn sergeant. *How...?* Sullivan felt a panic rip through him, while both horses tried to avoid a collision. Baby saw the old man's familiar wooly mustache curved above a desperate frown, and then he saw the sergeant raise his Sharpes buffalo gun with one hand and swing it toward his head. Baby ducked but felt the swish knock off his cap.

They were riding nearly on top of each other now, side by side. Tunneson tried again to knock Baby out of his saddle, but this time the kid's horse swerved away. They were making a great cloud of dust now, and Sullivan could hear the sergeant bellowing at him to stop. *He wants to take me back to hang*, he thought. *Like hell.* Steadying himself in the saddle, Baby felt the butt of his pistol and drew it out of its holster. Turning, he leveled it at Tunneson, but at the last second his aim faltered and he missed. They continued on, riding like devils out of the purple dawn, the lusty grunts of the horses the only sound.

Tunneson glared savagely at the form riding beside him, and for a fateful moment he forsook a lifetime of cavalry maneuvering skills, of clear-headedness, and the absence of hatred for the enemy. Even in the early days of Indian fighting, he tried to refrain from bitterness. But now, for the first time, he was in full gallop against an enemy he detested, a youthful braggart who just yesterday helped kill men in his patrol. Ahead too, where this trail ended, was the face of a woman. For that instant he let his mind blink, and with one last desperate aim of his pistol, Baby Sullivan fired another bullet, this time hitting Tunneson in the upper leg. The bullet, poorly aimed but lethal, passed through the sergeant's leg and into the belly of his racing horse. The animal ran for several yards before crumbling to the ground, throwing Tunneson hard onto the dirt trail. He rolled over and over like a tumbling ragdoll before coming to a crumbled stop in the sage. The last thing he saw before losing consciousness was the disappearing shadow of Baby Sullivan as he rode away.

Cletus Burke and the others heard the gunshots clearly as they followed in a pack. It was Finn O'Clery, riding in the lead, who saw the kid's kepi lying in the middle of the trail. He did not stop, hoping they would find the damn kid's boastful body next. But what they found, half a mile farther, was the form of their nemesis, Sergeant Lancelot Tunneson, stretched face down in the dust.

The pack swerved to avoid trampling him, then slowed to a

breathless stop. Burke dismounted first, pistol drawn, and crept with caution toward the prostate body. Turning him over, the deserter gave a whoop. "Well, I'll be a sonofabitch. If it ain't the root of all our problems bleeding to death before our very eyes." Several of the others jumped from their horses and gathered around, staring in disbelief.

"You think that dumb-ass kid did this?" O'Clery said, taking off his cap and scratching his head.

"Couldn't a' been no other," Burke answered. "Hell. Couldn't a' been mor'n five minutes ago."

"Is he dead?" This from Pup Murphy.

Burke studied Tunneson, just then stirring. "He ain't dead. But I reckon he'll wanna be pretty damn quick."

O'Clery and Quinn exchanged glances. Will Byrnes remained silent, angered and confused by his missing pistol.

Pup Murphy, still mounted, spied Tunneson's dead horse lying in the brush and hollered out. Burke wandered into the growing light to where the horse lay, and then gave another whoop. "Well, if this ain't the luck o' the Irish. That crazy old top sergeant was carrying a rope. If that don't beat all." He unleashed the rope from the saddle and, walking back tossed, it to O'Clery. "Cinch that thing around that bastard's ankles. Good and tight. I'm for giving him a ride into Peacock's store. Special delivery."

His laugh carried through the sagebrush like the squawk of a vulture.

Chapter 4

HENRY MUSSEL HAD JUST emerged from his tipi by the side of the corrals when he saw the horseman riding toward him out of the sun. Always the first to rise, he squinted at the racing form, riding hard, straight at him, when he felt a sharp pain in his chest. The sound of the gunshot came an instant later. Henry Mussel spun crazily and sat down on the ground, his brain fighting against closure. Before falling backward, he saw that the man was a soldier.

The gunfire brought Peacock stumbling through the front door of his store, still in his long underwear. He peered unknowingly into the yard. Baby Sullivan's second shot hit the old man in the belly. "Hi-ho!" Baby shouted. *Here is my destiny*, he thought. *I've killed myself an Injun, at last.* He spun his horse in a circle and stared into the corral where a dozen horses were stamping nervously.

From the tipi that stood next to Henry Mussel's tipi, appeared the form of Bull Head, another young Indian kept there by Peacock to help break the mustangs. In an instant he put it Peacock. He saw Henry lying near the bottom rail of the corral, then he saw the wild soldier shooting. He had no weapon, only an old, ornamental spear that he always kept as a decoration by the flap of his tipi. He grabbed it, almost absently, and taking one last look at Henry, he rushed the horseman, spear-point extended. He nearly made it before Baby turned and saw the Indian rushing him. With an uncharacteristic move of smooth deflection he batted the spear away at the last second, and at point blank put a bullet into the throat of Bull Head. The young Indian fell dead, the spear clattering to the hard-packed ground.

For a moment the yard fell silent, save for the frenzied horses in the corral. Then he heard a step on the store's porch and he turned to see a woman kneeling by the fallen Peacock. She was older, and she looked Indian, so that was good Peacock for Baby. Never a marksman, he missed his next two shots, the lead hitting the doorframe, throwing splintered wood. By this time the woman had dragged Peacock inside again, and slammed the door shut. An instant later a rifle barrel jutted out from an open window and fired.

Baby Sullivan spun his horse in a flash of fear. Here was something new for him. The ambush on Tunneson's patrol had been so sudden and so effective, there had been no return fire. But this, he did not like. Even as another bullet whistled above his head, he searched frantically for a place to take cover. The barn shed, on the far end of the corrals seemed too far to reach, so he dismounted and dove behind a horse trough, his courage draining from him.

As if in a well-rehearsed theater production, the sound of Burke's horses suddenly pounded into the yard. The rifleman in the store, perhaps thinking these were their rescuers, ceased firing. Burke called his men to a halt and sat surveying the scene before him. He stared at Sullivan with a resigned curiosity. His own dark deed lay at the end of a rope, bloodied and dead. He might have condemned this idiot kid, but now had no basis for condemnation. He dismounted, and walking back to the torn-up body of Sergeant Tunneson, he spat. "What the hell," he said. "Now we're murderers."

In the next instant, Private Will Byrnes fled from his horse in fright by another shot from the hidden rifleman. This time every pistol among them was laid to bear on the open window until all was quiet in the store.

Boone Crowe saw the distant thread of black smoke around noon, and judged it to be another half day's ride. He also knew where it was coming from and his stomach took a sick turn. He was too late. As much as he hated to, he climbed down from the saddle and led the Ghost Horse into a patch of shade and went searching for water. He found a shallow tarn of buffalo water a ways off and eventually took the horse to it. While the critter drank, Crowe watched the horizon where the smoke continued to trail higher into the air.

Crowe thought. It was not likely Lancelot Tunneson would set the trading post on fire. That too meant doubly bad news. Where was Lance? The ex-marshal's mood darkened. He drew his palm across his whiskered cheek. And where was Straw Dog? He had lost that crafty Indian's trail earlier in the morning. He waited another half hour, then put the saddle back on the Ghost Horse, and rode toward the smoke, a new urgency upon him.

The trading post was a mere pile of fallen timbers and smoldering black ash when he finally reached the knoll overlooking the place. Dusk was settling on a day completely underserving of its throaty pink and yellow beauty. His mind had been full of memories of his years scouting with Tunneson in the remote parts of Indian country in New Mexico territory, Utah, and finally Montana. In the War of the States, Tunneson had been at Gettysburg while Crowe was at Vicksburg, but their many hours of desert wanderings afterward gave them a trust that only such survivors could share. It wasn't a telling of old war stories; it was simply knowing that the other had been there and through it.

The scene before him was grisly. The trading post a charred shell and a standing tipi next to a burned circle in the ground where another tipi had once stood. The corral was empty of stock, save for the murdered carcasses of the army mounts that had carried the deserters here. As he drew closer he saw that there was a man in a sitting position, leaning against a fence rail, a spear driven in so deeply it was coming out the back. He sat and studied the gruesome sight. The man's face was destroyed, and his clothes torn to shreds. But even with all that, Crowe knew that it was his friend.

His war-accustomed eyes took in the surroundings a section at a time, trying to make sense of every detail. He had no desire to be a careless victim at the hands of a sniper's bullet. But with

29

the exception of the three cottonwood trees that wove into a cluster one hundred yards off, there was no place for a sniper to hide. Crowe finally dismounted and set about the gruesome task before him—taking an inventory of the dead, primarily that of Lancelot Tunneson. He stood for a long time at a distance, bracing himself against the hideous butchery, feeling his blood turn to boiling. He took off his hat and threw it on the ground, then both hands swiped at his eyes. Death was nothing new to the old battle-hardened marshal, but this was different.

Stepping to his old friend, Boone Crowe rolled Tunneson onto his side, and with shaking hands, broke off the tip of the spear where it exited the sergeant's back. Then, gripping the shaft with two hands, he slowly withdrew the bloodied spear until it was free. Tunneson's destroyed face left no great question in Crowe's mind—he'd been dragged behind a horse, feet first, leaving his face to be torn to bits. He's seen it done before with similar results. It was his hope that Lance was dead before they put the spear to him.

The likelihood of finding burying tools in a burnt down trading post seemed impossible, but returning to his hat, he beat the dust out of it and thrust it on his head. The half-charred bodies of Peacock and his wife were easy to see, lying just inside the burned-out store's threshold. The blackened body of another person lay curled in the still smoldering ash of the building. The stench of burned flesh brought the war back to him in vivid repulsion. Looking closely he saw that both Peacock and his wife had taken bullets. That left the other body, the burnt one, and through deduction he knew it must be the woman called Turtle. She had been a tall, handsome woman, a Shoshone or Crow, if he remembered right. He also knew something else about her— Lancelot Tunneson was in love with her. As far back as their last meeting, a year ago, Lance had confessed his skittish attempts at wooing her. She was a proud, beautiful woman, and Lance had said, *I'm a damn coward, Boone, when it comes to women. Give me a good artillery barrage and I'm okay. But this business of setting myself upon a woman, hell, I'm terrified.*

The deserters were more than that now; they were murderers. Murderers of the most brutal kind. From everything he could deduct, they had found Tunneson coming on the place and somehow managed to subdue him. They dragged him here and finished him off. The two Peacocks were easy prey. As for the two tipis, he knew nothing. Only that there had once been two and now there was only one. A lean-to horse shed had been pulled down, probably when the deserters traded their spent army horses for fresh mounts. Crowe took the killing of the army horses as a message to whoever came after—don't follow us. It was a message he had no intention of heeding. He knew already that he would follow them. And he would kill them.

Kicking through the broken-down horse shed he found his first break—a shovel. It was a flat-faced shovel for scooping up manure, but it would serve for the burying that laid ahead. It would take him the rest of daylight to accomplish, and he hated that every hour spent in burying, the murderers were getting farther away. But it was the last honor he could give to good people. He took the shovel and leaned it against a corral rail then removed the saddle from the Ghost Horse and led it toward the copse of cottonwoods where a stream cut through the grass. Even the birds seemed to have added a sad refrain to the death-filled day. Up here where the soil was soft was where he would bury Tunneson and the others. He would work into darkness, but it would be done proper, and then, by morning, he'd be on a trail of revenge.

Suddenly, above the birdsong, Boone Crowe heard a sound. It too had a melodic pitch, but it was not a bird. From long habit, his old army Colt was in his hand, and he approached the trees cautiously. The Ghost Horse's ears perked up and both man and horse listened. Getting closer, Boone knew it for what it was— an Indian death chant. He crept closer, and there, sitting cross-legged on the grassy bank of the stream, an adorned deer-skin poncho over her shoulders, and almost ghost-like in the shadowy

31

gloaming, was an Indian girl. Clutched in her hands was an ugly buffalo-skinning knife. Her chanting had covered his approach, and so now he was faced with a decision—how to cause no further harm by making himself known.

To his knowledge, suicide was not a common Indian practice. But self-mutilation might be. It was with the Comanche when he fought near Mexico. Still, that knife was a menacing weapon, and he had no desire to join Tunneson in the grave. Not yet. He had killing to do. Then, in the course of his pondering, he saw the girl's eyes open. They were dark as onyx stones but surprisingly they carried no fear. It was something deeper than fear, more akin to the same feelings Crowe felt himself—a clear mind for vengeance. *How does she fit into this?* he wondered. He held the pistol high, then in full view returned it to its holster. Was it something in his own tormented face that allowed her, after a long minute, to return the gesture by laying her knife in the grass beside her?

The girl's chanting stopped and the birdsong returned.

The six deserters, on fresh horses, thundered first westward for two hours, then turned toward the north. By dark they made a hasty camp in the cleft of a dry river wash, the lust of murder still upon them. Baby Sullivan, almighty crazed by having killed himself an Indian at last, continued hooting like a crowing cock-roster. He flung himself from his newly acquired mount and threw his head back with a laugh. "You shoulda seen how easy it was. That damn Injun was dead afore he could even give a whoop."

L. P. Quinn ignored him, dismounting and moved away from the others. He would just as soon have killed Baby himself just to shut him up. He made a spot against the dry bank and tended to his horse. Finn O'Clery was patting the kid on the back. "Yer pa woulda been proud of ye, Baby. Keepin the Sullivan name alive."

To this Cletus Burke merely grunted. It had been a long day, and there were still things that needed hashing out.

By nightfall Pup Murphy had built a fire and put together a fine supper from supplies they'd stolen from the trading post—eggs, bacon, and cans of peaches. They gathered around the fire and ate from tin plates, more of the bounty, and filling up on whisky O'Clery had found in a cellar at the post. There was plenty to go around, and everybody took their turns, drinking from the neck of the bottle. All except Private Will Byrnes, who had not spoken a word since they'd left the killing field.

Finally Cletus Burke spoke. "Me ain't leavin here with any of you in the morning. I'll be goin at it alone. And I reckon you'd be wise to do the same."

"Well, I'll be glad to be shed of ya anyway," blurted Baby. "You ain't got no measure on me anymore no how."

"I'm plumb feelin the same as Burke," chimed in O'Clery. "I'm fixin to go it alone."

"Well ain't you a fine bunch," continued Baby. "I ain't under Burke's thumb no more. But I figured I'd like a little company. What about you, L. P.? Wanna team up?"

"You wouldn't like it, Baby. I fear it would be a short ride for you."

Baby stiffened, noting the glint in Quinn's smiling eyes. "What about you, Pup?"

Pup Murphy made no answer, and when all eyes fell on Private Byrnes, he simply stared into the fire.

"To hell with all of you, then. I'll go set the world on fire all by my lonesome then."

"You do that, Baby," Cletus Burke said, nodding. "Have at it."

O'Clery let out a roar of drunken laughter. "How's this for a wager? What say we all meet up someplace, say, in a year from now? We could meet up Canada way. Or San Francisco. How's that? Might be entertainin to see who makes it. And who don't."

"I'd make it," Baby hollered.

O'Clery laughed. "And yer the very one I bet don't make it.

Not with that mouth of yers. Someone's like to cut yer tongue out afore the passing of another month."

Suddenly everything turned tense, and Baby let his hand drop to the butt of his pistol. But O'Clery shut him up with a word. "Anytime." No one else spoke, but eyes darted back and forth across the firelight, waiting for something to happen. Finally O'Clery laughed. "I'd sure hate to bloody that brand-new checkered shirt of yers, Baby. It looks right smart on ye." He nodded slowly, smiling. "You wear that shirt next year when you get to San Francisco. I wanna see how many bullet holes it has in it by then."

Nobody intervened because most of them wished O'Clery would just kill the kid. But the issue was settled when Baby Sullivan stood up and wordlessly staggered to where his horse was picketed and saddled it. In a drunken slur he bid his former company adieu, and, missing the stirrup twice before managing to get his boot in it, he mounted awkwardly. With a wave of a drunken arm, he rode into the darkness, the echo of hoof beats finally fading away.

After a while, Cletus Burke said to O'Clery, "I wouldn't ride the same way when you set out. He's got yer number."

O'Clery nodded, but added, "The kid won't last the month."

Chapter 5

It was near midnight when the burying was finished. The graves were not deep but deep enough, Tunneson buried with the burnt corpse of the woman, Turtle, which seemed fitting, giving them a togetherness in death. They also put Peacock and his wife together in a grave. The young Indian buck, Bull Head was buried alone. The body of Henry Mussel was not found in the dark, and this seemed to grieve the girl heavily, though she spoke not of it. The last thing Crowe did was knot Tunneson's cavalry neckerchief around the charred scrap of wood he used as a marker. It was the best he could do.

They had worked side by side, and mostly without words, but when the girl did speak, Boone Crowe was surprised by the girl's near-perfect English, but he said nothing. He gauged her to be about nineteen or twenty, and not Crow like the Turtle woman, rather Cheyenne. Peacock's own wife was Cheyenne, which might mean this girl was kin of some sort. Every now and then he stole a glance at her while he dug with the shovel. Her long, black hair hung loose, but he guessed it was from the ordeal rather than Cheyenne fashion. Boone wanted to know everything about what happened, and it would have to come soon, before he left at first light. He hated to leave her here alone, but he had to get back on the track of the killers.

They sat facing each other. Neither was hungry, not after the gruesome task they had just finished, but they forced themselves to share jerked meat from Crowe's saddlebags. He chewed and looked into the depth of her dark eyes. "You speak good English."

She lifted her gaze. "White man's school."

Crowe nodded. "Orphan?"

"Willow Creek."

The old marshal frowned.

The girl studied him, watching his eyes, waiting for his words. But when he didn't say anything, she spoke again. "You were there," she said. "I saw you. You were on a big horse. A black horse."

Hunter, he thought. "That was ten years ago." His words were low, husky with regret.

"I know. I was only ten. Ten winters. But I saw you." She looked away for a moment, then she looked at him again, her eyes narrowing, like the eyes of a snake. Was she about to coil and strike? "You were shouting at the soldier men. Shouting at them to stop. You used your big pistol…" She stopped here and pointed at his army Colt that was shoved into his holster. "I saw you use your pistol to hit a soldier man. He was trying to kill my people. And you were trying to stop him."

She fell silent then, putting both palms on her face, covering her eyes. She didn't need her eyes to see it again. It was stenciled on her memory.

Boone Crowe saw it now too, as if it were still happening around them. He had scouted the column there. But not to kill anybody. They were there to talk to Red Knife. They were there to take a head count, nothing more. Part of the government's silly idea of taking a census of the Cheyenne who had settled peacefully in the area. Inventorying a nomadic people? It made no sense. But it was a green lieutenant—Glavin—jittery as a rabbit. Something happened. Something always happened. The shooting came with a mighty explosion.

"You tried to stop it," the girl finally said again.

Crowe heaved a long, deep breath. "What else did you see?"

"I saw my parents killed."

The old marshal closed his eyes.

"And I saw you kill the soldier man. The one with the long knife. I saw you yelling at him to stop. I saw him raise his long knife, and I saw you put your pistol—that pistol—into his face. I saw you shoot him dead. He fell from his horse, and I saw your horse walk on him."

The fire burned low but neither noticed. They sat for a long time in silence. Finally Boone Crowe looked at the girl. "How could you remember such a horrible thing?"

She returned his gaze. "How could I forget such a horrible thing?"

Of course, he thought. The girl's Willow Creek was the same as his Vicksburg. It was the same as his Cold Harbor and Wilderness fight. All the things from the War of the States that still haunted him were branded into her memory in the form of Willow Creek.

"It was the last thing I ever did for the army. You might be the only other person that knows I am guilty of murdering an army officer." He let his hand move to his chin where graying whiskers stood out like thorny prickly pear. "Is that why you weren't afraid of me when I found you here at the cottonwoods?"

"I saw you coming. And I knew."

Crowe drew in a mighty breath. "So they shipped you off to a school."

"Omaha," she said. "I was there a long time. I ran away many times. But they always brought me back. They called me Isabel. But my name is Iron Hand." She held out her right hand, and even in the dim light Crowe could see the long scar across her palm. "When I was a little child, I touched the iron cooking kettle that was on the fire. It burned me. After that, I was Iron Hand."

"How did you get back here?"

"Uncle Pea sent for me. He said I had been gone long enough."

"How did you know Peacock?"

"His wife is...*was,* my mother's sister. She was there at Willow Creek too." Her face turned dark again. "They raped Turtle. Those men. They killed Uncle Pea and my aunt. They put on new clothes. Drank whisky. Killed their horses."

Boone Crowe felt edgy. "I have to find these men. You must know that. I have to kill them. They murdered my friends. I have their names right here. They are written on this paper." He removed the crumbled sheet from his shirt pocket, unfolded it, and read off the names. "Cletus Burke. L. P. Quinn. A man named Byrnes. Another named Murphy. Finn O'Clery. And a kid named Baby. Baby Sullivan."

She let the sound of Crowe's voice settle around her, then she said in a quiet tone, "I will go with you."

Crowe shook his head. "That can't happen."

Iron Hand's jaw set. "I will."

"They will be scattering now. That's what fugitives do. I know that because I've tracked many when I was a marshal."

"And how will you find them."

"I have their names."

"And I have better than names." She looked hard into his eyes. "I have their faces. Your names are worthless without their faces. I will go with you. I will never forget their faces. Just like I never forgot yours."

Under a yellow moon, a coyote padded across an open stretch of prairie, head bent low, following a much-traveled trail to her den. Suddenly it stopped. A strange scent in the wind caught her attention. The animal pressed itself to the ground and sniffed. There was blood in the air too, and the coyote crept closer, nose up, following the trace.

In the moonlight, there was something curled in front of the coyote's den, and at first her lips pulled back in a snarl, but the head dipped lower, and as she approached, the danger lessening. Her pups were lying on top of what she knew to be a man, and they were not molesting it, rather licking it. The man was an Indian, for she knew the familiar lusty smell of their skin, and in her coyotes' mind, she believed he was dead.

She had no fear now, even though she heard the man breathing.

Boone Crowe woke, feeling old as the mountains. Gray light showed through the base of the tipi, but he could see that the girl, Iron Hand, was gone. Somehow he had managed to sleep on his sidearm, and now he felt his hip complain as he tried to stand.

Sleeping on the ground was not meant for old men, he realized. He found his hat and stepped through the flap into a predawn morning. He took in the bitter sight of the massacre and the fire, hoping it wasn't so, but there was no wiping it away, so he spit on the ground.

He heard a noise and looking up saw the girl rummaging through the ashes of the burnt-out trading post. In the gray mist she looked like a vapor. He watched her for a while as she kicked through the blackened debris, her head down as if looking for something. The light, this early, wasn't much better than it was last night when they set to burying the dead.

"Hey," he said.

The girl looked up.

"What are you looking for?"

"Money."

Crowe scratched the whiskers on his cheek. "Money?"

She didn't answer him but fell on her knees and scratched through the charred wood and earth. The coals were no longer hot, so she clawed like a dog searching for a bone.

Boone Crowe moved closer.

The girl let out a light humming. "Here. It's here." She dug until she lifted up a small metal box with both hands. She waved it in the air, creating a jingling sound as if it were some sort of music box.

He watched her walk out of the rubble, her knees black with soot, and set the box down on the ground in front of him. A padlock secured it.

"Shoot it," she demanded. "Shoot off the lock."

"Are you robbing the dead?"

"Uncle Pea always hid spare money in here. When there was any. I saw him do it. Shoot it. Hurry. We must get going."

He thought for a minute he might still be sleeping, that this was a strange dream. Finally, he told the girl to get away, and pulling his ugly war Colt from its holster, he pulled the trigger and watched the metal box jump like a bull frog and land upside down, a cascade of coins spreading and spinning on the ground.

Without a word, Crowe stood and watched as the girl knelt and picked up the coins, palming them into a beaded, leather pouch that was strung over her shoulder. Finally he said, "You planning on opening a bank?"

She looked up at him. "I'm planning on buying a horse. And if there is enough money, a rifle." She gave him what came close to a sneer. "We can't ride double on that pale horse of yours forever."

"I have a rifle," he said. "A Henry."

"I saw it. Your horse is all saddled and ready to go. I've just been waiting for you to wake up."

"And where do you plan on buying a horse?"

"Any place I can."

Boone Crowe knew most of the towns in all directions from here. He had chased down outlaws in many of them. The men he was after could be in any one of them by now. So, where to start? There was Ludlow to the east. The hamlet of Dog Run to the south. Farther south was Laramie and Cheyenne, but they were too big. Not a place deserters likely wanted to be seen. Not yet. *West or north most likely*, he reasoned. He'd hoped to make short work of this, but even now, time was being wasted.

The girl was looking at him, so he simply pointed to the Ghost Horse and told her to get on. As they rode away from the killing field, Boone Crowe took one last look at the graves, and his blood felt hot in his veins. Even when he wore the badge of United States Territorial Marshal, he had done some things that weren't marshal-like. But Rud Lacrosse wore the badge now. One of his oldest and best friends was buried in the ground here. Ahead, he knew, lay the revenge trail, and he vowed to find the murderers and kill them, law or no law.

One by one, the remaining five deserters left the campsite,

most nursing hangovers from the whisky-laced bluster of their murderous rampage. They exchanged very few words, and after a half hour, they were all out of sight from one another. Pup Murphy and Will Byrnes rode together, heading southwest, harboring no idea of where that direction might take them. Cletus Burke, sporting a wide sombrero and a blue-metal revolver stolen from the Peacock store, rode due west, straight for the wide open.

"If I ever see any of you again, I hope it's at your funeral," Burke said, departing.

No one laughed. They watched Burke take off at a gallop, each wondering if a bullet in Burke's back might be a fitting farewell. It had been Burke who finally killed the Crow woman. After everyone except Byrnes had taken their turn with her, it was O'Clery who wanted to keep her for himself. But, out of mercy or out of bloodlust, Burke put a bullet in her head.

O'Clery turned to L. P. Quinn and they shook hands. "Whichever of us kills that sonofabitch, be sure to cut off his ears. The other buys the drinks."

They saddled their mounts in silence, then O'Clery spoke. "You got a plan?"

"New York tis east. I was thinkin bout going back." Quinn's Irish broch was still thick from last night's whisky, his tongue tight and heavy.

"I'm done with all that. My eyes 'er on San Francisco. By way of Cheyenne's railhead."

The two men sized each other up. Seeing each other in stolen civilian clothes for the first time, they paused for a moment in marvel. Then, as in concert, they both patted their pistols with open palms. "Best to ya, Quinn," O'Clery said. In another minute they had mounted, and with one final wave of their hats, they rode away in opposite directions.

Chapter 6

THE ADDED BURDEN of the Cheyenne girl did not alter the steady pace of the Ghost Horse, as the two doubled-up riders rode with the sun at their backs. The initial departing tracks of the deserters were plain as a road map in the upturned grass and red clay. In time this trail would lead to where the killers had camped last night, but Boone Crowe was sure they would find it empty, its occupants having scattered. There was light morning mist hanging in the dips of the land, and the old marshal kept a close eye out for a possible ambush from mere habit, though they likely believed they had killed anyone who might have been able to follow.

Last night, in the tipi, as he and the girl sat before the small fire, she had explained how she'd survived. When Peacock had heard the first gunshot, he'd told her to hide in a well-concealed broom closet. From there, shaking with fear, which eventually turned to hatred, she saw everything that had transpired afterward. She'd heard the pistol shots that killed her uncle and aunt, but the Crow woman, Turtle, hollered for her to stay hidden. From there, through a crack in the wallboards, she saw it all. *I almost fainted,* she'd said. *But I thought about the Indian school. How I had to teach myself to remember the white man's numbers. The white man's letters. So I kept looking. I can still see their faces.*

After they had killed the Crow woman, they refashioned themselves with trousers and shirts from the store. They filled up on food, whisky, and ammunition and set the building on fire. Through the smoke and flames, Iron Hand had escaped from her closet and out the back door. From her place up by the grove of trees, where Crowe had found her, she witnessed the killing of the army horses. *I still hear their screams,* she said. *And the men laughing.*

Boone Crowe let all of this replay in his mind. *These men are a rare breed of evil,* he thought. Rud Lacrosse had spoken once about the hyenas of Africa and how they lurked around campfires,

43

slinking ever closer for the kill, snarling the whole time. Lacrosse had shown him a picture in a book of a hyena, and so now Crowe found himself attaching that image to the murderers' faces. He planned to look into those faces and study them, if only for a moment before killing them.

By midday they came across the camp and the trash that was left behind—a still-warm fire, a scattering of whisky bottles and cans of beans and pemmican, and a mad cluster of hoof prints departing in all different directions. Crowe kicked through the junk for only a few minutes, letting the horse and girl rest, then he remounted and they continued on. An hour later they saw a man in the distance, piling hay ricks in a field. As they approached, the man stood watching them, his pitching fork held in his hand.

The man, in overalls and sporting a silver beard, tilted back his straw hat and stared up at the two riders. Though the girl was wearing the tan trousers of a white boy, on top she wore a leather fringed poncho, her black hair, tied in long, twisted braids made it clear she was not a boy, but an Indian girl. And Crowe, in his high-crowned hat and drooping, grayish mustache, made them a sight of curiosity to the farmer.

"I stand out here in my field and do not spy another livin soul for near on a month." Chuckling, the farmer waved off a horsefly pestering his face. "But today…why, dammed if you ain't the third. Makes a workin man want to stop…thinkin he missed a holiday."

Crowe felt the girl tighten her hold on him from behind. "Who and when?" he asked.

"Can't say about who. But the when was jist after sunup. Headin hell bent."

"To where?"

The farmer pointed with his pitchfork. "Thata way. Tracks is easy to follow. You on the hunt, mister?"

Crowe ignored the question.

"Have you a horse to sell?" the girl asked, her English startling the old farmer.

44

Recovering, he shook his head. "You wouldn't want my old nag. But they sure to have a hoss down in Dog Run. I think that's where those other fellers was headin."

Crowe tipped his hat, and in another half an hour they could see the scattered buildings of Dog Run nestled in a notch of a side hill.

"I don't much like bein here," Will Byrnes said. "I don't much like bein anywhere."

"Well, that don't make much sense, Will," Pup Murphy answered. "Ya can't be everywhere and ya can't be nowhere. So here's where ya be. Make the best of it."

Byrnes' brows were knitted. He did not have a hat. He only had a new stripped shirt and pants because they were thrust on him by O'Clery at the trading post. That whole affair had sickened him. Even now he wished he'd never run away from the army. He'd been led into running away because Burke liked to order him to. Burke had once been like an uncle to him. Way back, it was Burke who got him to leave the city and join him in the army. And now Burke was up and gone. Without him.

Pup was not interested in Byrnes' misery. His eyes were on the gal sitting with the piano player across the smoky, near-empty room of the dingy saloon. A closer look would have shown the hard miles on her face, but Pup was too far away to notice, and too filled with whisky to care. It had been Pup who drew the first card with the Crow woman, and he was itching for more now. The woman, in her vast experience, was well aware of Pup Murphy, and after a few more minutes of teasing, she would stroll on over and introduce her best action on him.

Will Byrnes rose from the table and wandered over to the filmy window and gazed out at the livery stable across the dusty street. He wondered what would happen if he slipped away and rode back to the fort. He could turn himself in. When someone found out about the trading post, and the killings, he could say he wasn't any part of it. He'd say he didn't know what they was talking about. But then he remembered that other fellow, the one who got shot for deserting. *No,* he thought, *I can't go back.*

He heard Pup whoop, and turning around he saw the saloon gal siting on Pup's lap. She had knocked off his hat and was putting her fingers through his curly hair. Pup was giggling like a school boy, so Will turned back to the window. Maybe he should leave and not care where he went. Just get away from Pup. But he was afraid. Will Byrnes was always afraid of something. Now, beyond the livery stable, to the surrounding hills, he saw a horse coming down through the trail, leaving a trail of dust. It was one horse with two riders. An old man and a girl.

"Hold down the fort, old pard," Murphy howled.

Byrnes turned in time to see the gal waltzing Pup up the stairs, the whore's hand already groping in Pup's back pocket. Byrnes felt the heat of confusion. It was like a panic. The same panic he had when they first rode away from Fort Laramie. And the panic when they killed Sergeant Tunneson. He had felt numb and afraid ever since. The killings at the trading post were like sleepwalking. A horrible kind of nightmare.

Back at the window he saw that the old man and girl were now in the street. Even in Will's addled mind, he thought it an odd pair, riding together like that. The horse was so pale it appeared invisible. He watched as the girl slid off the back of the horse. When she straightened, he saw that she was young and an Indian. The old man was saddle-worn but carried himself with a peculiar authority. He took the horse to the water trough and let it drink. The girl looked around with sharp, hawkish eyes. There was something about both of them that set Byrnes' hands to shaking.

Watching, it looked to Byrnes as if the girl and the old man were having a discussion. Even an argument. Apparently the man won because the girl looked angrily at him, glaring across the saddle at the man as he turned and headed toward the very saloon Byrnes was watching from. But even as the batwing doors swung open, Will Byrnes saw the girl's eyes lock on his through the window glass. He didn't know why, but terror filled him.

Boone Crowe stood in the doorway for a moment, letting his eyes adjust from the bright sun to the dim interior. The piano man was still pounding out a meaningless tune, and the barkeep tapped his fingers absently to the broken melody. Crowe moved close and motioned for the barkeep. "How cold's the beer?"

"It's drinkable. You want?"

Crowe nodded. As he waited he glanced at the young man at the window, noticing the edgy way he tilted back and forth. The beer came and he spoke to the barkeep. "That fellow have a tremor of some kind?"

The barkeep shrugged. "His friend just went upstairs with Faye. But this here fellow, he looks a wreck. Can't say why, though."

"How long they been here?"

"You the law or something?"

Boone Crowe risked a nod.

"Couple of hours."

"Names?"

The barkeep laughed. "Drifters don't give names."

Crowe took a long drink from his beer, then nodded. "Mighty good," he said. "Now, a question."

"Another one?"

"Yes, another one. Do you have an objection to me bringing my niece in here? She's Cheyenne."

The barkeep laughed. "Now that's a hell of a question. Of course I have an objection. Niece or not, I don't serve Injuns."

"I never said anything about serving her. It's just, well, it's just been a hell of a ride. I think just sittin on one of them chairs there for a spell. Why it might please her."

"I don't give a horse's ass if it would please her." His face reddened.

"Okay. I was just askin. Don't get all renegade on me now."

47

He turned his back on the barkeep and continued to drink his beer. After a while he put his mug back on the bar and slowly walked toward the door. As he did he tried to catch Byrnes' eye, but the young deserter was still staring through the window.

Outside, the girl stood alongside the Ghost Horse, glaring at Byrnes. Crowe went to her. "What's the verdict?"

"He's one of them," she said.

"You sure?"

Iron Hand glared at Crowe.

"Okay. There's another one upstairs getting entertained. Who do you think this other one might be? I need to be sure they're together. The barman said they came in together, but this one here," he tilted his head toward the window, "he's a bag of nerves."

"This one was there. But he stood back through most of it. He's a rabbit. The other one…" She shrugged. "There was another young one, like him. But…he…he was the first one to… with Turtle." She tilted her chin in the direction of the two horses tied to a hitching rail. "Those are Uncle Pea's. I saw them ride away. This one in the window was on the bay. The appaloosa carried the other young one."

Crowe looked at her. "We can't afford a mistake here."

"The other one had a mark on his face. Right here," she said, touching a place on her right cheek, just below the eye. "Something…like a black, flat mole." Her voice was clipped with hatred.

"Okay. You keep an eye on this one. I think I'll wander upstairs and have a word with Faye and her lover."

The girl looked at Crowe through dark, angry eyes. "Don't wait too long."

Boone Crowe walked past the nervous Will Byrnes, and when he put his boot on the first groaning step of the stairs, the barkeep looked up. "Hey, you can't—"

The old marshal's army Colt came up, putting an end to the barkeep's protest. "You and Mister Piano there. Pour yourselves a drink. On me. I'll square up in two minutes." He watched for a moment longer to make sure no shotgun appeared from behind the bar, then he moved up the stairs. His search was short, for the sound of howling and the squeaking of bedsprings filled the hallway.

Boone Crowe took a breath. He felt his blood rising. He turned the knob and swung open the door. Faye had her back to him as he entered, and she was bouncing around on her victim as if at a rodeo. He pulled the hammer back on his Colt, and the sound stopped all movement. The whore, who may have had experience in such matters, turned and looked, first at the yapping barrel of the pistol and then at Crowe's face.

"Step away, Miss Faye."

She quickly obliged, moving her nakedness off the bed and wiggling it into a far corner, leaving a startled Pup Murphy with wide eyes. The black mark on his face shone like a talisman to his own undoing.

"Which one of you killed my friend?"

"Huh…what?"

"Sergeant Tunneson."

"Oh…*him*. It…wait, mister. It wasn't me. It…it was Burke who…"

The gleam in Lancelot Tunneson's eyes when he was confessing his affection for the Crow woman appeared in Crowe's mind. The sheepish stammering. The sudden youthful expression that betrayed an awkward admission to love. It was the happiest Boone had ever seen him. It was the face Crowe had hoped he would always remember. But the Lance Tunneson he last saw had no face. It had been dragged away by the brush and rocks at the end of a rope.

The war Colt blasted, and the bullet seemed almost to nail Pup Murphy to the wall. Blood spilled out below his chin, and a trail of blue smoke seeped from the end of Crowe's pistol barrel, now hot with the fire of revenge.

Faye was screaming, but Crowe didn't hear her. All other

things were blotted out. Then, suddenly, still standing there he heard the sound of his Henry firing downstairs. There was broken glass too and another warning shot. He knew the sound of his Henry. And he already knew what had happened. Finally moving down the stairs he saw the shattered window and the body of the nervous kid lying sprawled all akimbo on the floor. Both the barkeep and the piano man were bunched in a corner, faces pale, and hands held high above their heads.

"They were army deserters," Crowe said, looking at the two pathetic characters quaking on the floor. His own voice strangely calm. "They murdered Peacock and his wife up at the trading post. And they set it ablaze. They murdered Sergeant Tunneson and his woman. Any questions?"

Both men shook their heads.

Boone Crowe slapped a coin down on the bar top, then walked outside to the girl, his own hands beginning to shake.

Henry Mussel felt a weight on him. A warm weight. He laid still, trying to gauge the pain in his side. Any attempt to move seemed hopeless. There was fire in his head, the heat of fever. And on his back he could feel the up and down breathing of the coyote pups. It was no longer night, but the hole he had dragged himself into was dark. His grandfathers had been there with him, all of them, dancing and singing. All night long he had heard the rattle of their medicine sticks. The drums. The drums felt like the fire in his head.

They left Dog Run the same way they had come, back over the same trail. The girl was now astride the Appaloosa that her Uncle Pea had kept in the corrals, and the bay horse that Murphy and Byrnes had stolen, followed on a lead rope. Neither spoke

50

after the bloodshed. Iron Hand was still holding the Henry in her hands when Crowe emerged from the saloon, and so he took it from her and shoved it back in its saddle scabbard.

The sky was clear, and Boone Crowe watched the occasional hawk or raven circle above. Far to the east his wife, Rose of Sharon, was helping Yelena with the delivery of a child in Illinois. And only this morning two sons of mothers were killed. *The choices some people make,* he thought. A parade of images passed through his head, of the men he had killed in the line of duty. But murder, he knew, had many faces. The captain whom he killed at Willow Creek had been in the heat of battle, where alliances were formed in a split-second. But here? He had scarcely given this Pup Murphy a chance to explain. On this day, he wanted no explanations. He just wanted to start the killing. What would Rose think? Or Rud? Had he lost his sense of justice?

As he rode, he leaned forward and stroked a hank of the Ghost Horse's mane. Images of the dead came back to him, all the way back to Cold Harbor and the Wilderness, to the bodies of Lancelot and the two Peacocks. Justice too, like murder, has many faces. He would allow these deserters the same justice they allowed their victims. Two were dead now. One from his own gun and one from the girl's. Four remained.

He glanced at the Cheyenne girl riding beside him. Her face was set like flint. Was she having similar thoughts? She had been right, though. Without her, names would have been no good. He needed her memory of the faces. Of each man's defects. And he would need her still. He studied her. Long before Rose. And long before Eva, his lost love, there had been another, a woman he never spoke of. He did think about her, though, from time to time. That was one of the secrets that Lancelot and he shared, and why his friend's love for the Turtle woman solidified that secret.

This girl too was a Cheyenne—Cheyenne women being well-known for their beauty. Directly following the War of the States, Crowe had kept to the army, leaving the Pennsylvania farm to his aging father, and his brother, Ferris. Ferris had been wounded at Manassas and returned home with a permanent limp but still strong enough to follow a plow. Long before his years serving under General Nelson Miles in the southwest, Boone was assigned to an outpost along the Platte River, defending settlers moving west.

It was later, in a winter camp along the Yellowstone that a handful of Cheyenne braves and their women were captured and held as hostages. The whole Indian business was still new with no semblance of strategy for defeat or pacification. Only happenstance and chaos. After the war, many officers had to forfeit their wartime rank if returning to active duty. So Boone Crowe fell from a major back down to a sergeant. I was on a bitterly cold morning when a troop of soldiers brought in seven Cheyenne, five braves and two women. By midnight the following day, four of the five braves had escaped, a testament to early military knowledge of the Indians prowess.

Little Feet was younger even than Iron Hand, Crowe remembered. Iron Hand claimed twenty snows. At that time, Little Feet couldn't have been more than sixteen or seventeen, if that. But she was the most handsome young woman Boone had ever seen, red or white. She was kept under loose guard throughout the winter, and by spring Boone Crowe believed that a life with this Cheyenne maiden was all set before him. He was already thirty, or approaching it, but it mattered not.

Watching Iron Hand riding beside him made it easy to return his thoughts to Little Feet and the telling moment when he admitted his love for her. Kissing is a learned experience for Indians, and he set out to give her lessons. But youth and culture are not fair accomplices in the matter of love. One day, while on patrol, Sergeant Boone Crowe returned to the camp only to find that Little Feet had been put on a train to a reservation in the south. Try as he might, he never saw her again. They had lain together, and he could still recall the warmth of her body, but she now only lives in that memory. And here, in the girl Iron Hand, the memory came back.

Later, having returned to their original trail, Crowe and Iron Hand dismounted and studied the sky. It was barely noon.

"I didn't think we would find them so soon," the girl said. There was no regret in her voice.

Crowe was sober. "Could there have been a different way?"

She looked at him. "No! It was the best way. You did not see what I saw."

"In my life," he said, turning away from her, "I've seen plenty. And it's never a thing of beauty."

They let silence pass between them for a moment. Finally she asked, "Did your man upstairs die with honor?"

Boone shook his head. "No. He did not."

"Then he will face the afterworld with the same dishonor."

Chapter 7

BABY SULLIVAN SAT ON a round boulder and gazed at the land around him. He was hungry and had no food. In his stubborn flight from the camp the night before, he had thrown all sense of survival to the wind. Far in the distance he saw cattle grazing, but in his admitted stupidity, he wouldn't have the first idea of how to make a meal of a dead cow. Or a dead anything, rabbit or pronghorn. The army had fed him, clothed him, and tucked him down at night. It might have been beans and gravy and a scratchy wool blanket, but it was there before him every day.

He removed his army-issue pistol from its holster and cradled it in both hands. That too had been a mark of haste—he had only two bullets left and none in his belt. Two bullets in a land as wide and hard as anything he'd ever seen. This wasn't the same as being on patrol when an officer, or that damn Tunneson, was barking orders. Now he was on his own, and the feel of it was different then he imaged. Hell, he didn't even know the difference between north and south.

Putting his pistol away he lifted his canteen and shook it. At least he had that, but when it was empty, it would be as worthless as a pistol with no bullets. *I need to do some figurin*, he thought.

Scarcely two miles to the northwest of where Baby Sullivan sat pondering, Cletus Burke knew exactly where he was going. Unlike the kid, Burke did know his directions, and he knew that if he kept to the same bearing, he would end up in Montana. Also, he'd had the foresight to fill his saddlebags with a booty of food and ammunition. When he had finally arrived at the trading post, dragging Tunneson behind him, he saw that Baby Sullivan had already turned the place into hell. Both Peacock and his women lay dead at their very doorstep. And an Indian was sprawled in the yard. Baby had the look of crazed, almighty bloodlust in his eyes. He should have killed the kid that very moment. But then O'Clery joined in the savagery and so he let them have their fun.

Burke had had his own moment. The temptation of giving

Tunneson a slow death was an act of spontaneous rage. For once he was on the winning end. His hatred of the top sergeant had festered for a year after Tunneson had him stripped of his corporal stripes for disobeying an order in the field, and worse. Their small patrol had come upon an old Indian man burying his young daughter who'd died of cholera. He was alone, perched near a rocky crag, gently laying stones on his daughter's grave. Tunneson had sent Burke ahead to investigate. *Do no harm,* Tunneson had instructed. But even as the sergeant watched from a distance, he saw Burke raise his carbine and shoot the old man dead.

What followed was a sound beating at the hands of Tunneson. Riding up, he knocked Burke from his mount and then proceeded to thrash him there in the dust and rocks with the rest of the patrol watching in open astonishment. When the colonel heard the story, he busted Burke down to private on the grounds of disobeying an order. There was no mention of murder as part of the punishment. Burke's eyes were black, and his cheeks and lips were cracked and bleeding. Tunneson had already taken care of the murder charge.

Once whisky was found in the cellar of the trading post, there was no holding the men back, so lots were drawn for the Crow woman, and filled with whisky and lust, all but Byrnes had taken part. After pillaging the store's stock for clothes, ammunition, and food, it was time to find fresh mounts. It had been O'Clery who'd propped Tunneson up against the corral and shoved the spear through him for added measure. Then he set the place ablaze.

The Laramie range rose before him now, and he sat his horse for a moment and gloried in the scene. Awhile after leaving the others, heading west, he had turned his horse northward, where he knew were mountains beyond these. He'd listened to some of the old timers talking about a big river that came down out of Canada, bigger than the Platte and bigger than the Yellowstone. Maybe that's where he'd end up, after a spell in Montana. Wherever opportunity took him. He scratched at the beginnings of a beard with a hand missing a little finger, lost to the jaws of a vicious dog as a boy. He had long ago forgotten about it and found himself smiling into the distance. *Life is good,* he thought.

Dusk was moving in, and the flat, pink line of it stretched across the land in front of Henry Mussel. Lying at the cusp of the coyote den, he struggled to get back his wits. Still feverish, he stared at the horizon, trying to put back the pieces of how he had gotten here and how he'd been shot. In his delirium he kept seeing a man squatting in the distance, staring at him. One minute he would be there; the next minute he'd be gone. Now, as the day darkened, and the coyote pups again started their nuzzling and nosing about him, he saw the figure again. A man, one hundred yards away, like a medicine vision. His image waffled like a mirage in the warm eventide.

"If Straw Dog was here, he could tell me more." Boone Crowe was crouched low, examining the hoofmarks left by two horses. "Tracks tell stories," he continued, more or less to himself. Finally he stood and looked at the girl. "Obviously two riders. But not together. This set…" he pointed to where one horse had continued straight ahead, "this one was here first. By a couple of hours or more, I'd say." Turning, he let his eyes train on the other tracks, breaking off and leading slightly northward. "These came later."

She watched as he turned scenarios over in his mind.

"This first rider has a bigger lead on us. But he's not traveling fast. Neither is this other one."

"What does that mean?"

"It means they ain't worried much about bein followed."

"Even with the big fire?"

He looked at her. "It's a big country. Houses burn down every day."

"Will not the army want to know what happened to your sergeant friend?"

Boone Crowe considered this. "I might have thought so. Before I met Captain Gillespie."

"What does that mean?"

"Nothing. Just a hunch."

The girl showed impatience. "Which one, then?"

He tilted his hat back off his forehead. "There were two sets of tracks heading east too, remember?"

She stared at him with cold eyes.

"Look. I want these men as bad as you do. But we've got four men left, all traveling in different directions. It's a toss of the dice." He stood and kicked at the dirt. "Those two today came quick. Don't get a spoiled head on you now. Thinking it'll be that easy from here out. It won't."

Iron Hand frowned. "What is a toss of the dice?"

"It's…a shot in the dark. You don't know what you might hit. If you hit anything. The luck of the draw."

She shook her head, confused.

"It doesn't matter. All I'm saying is, whichever trail we chose to follow, we'll find them. But it's going to be one at a time from here on out. And that takes time. So, pick your poison."

"Poison?"

Crowe shook his head. "What did they teach in that Omaha school anyway?"

"How to read." She said this with bitterness.

"I think east. Call it a hunch, but I think if we go back to where they camped and follow that set of tracks heading east, we'll catch them. If we don't, they have the whole damn country to hide in. From here all the way to President Arthur's doorstep."

"Another hunch? What about these?" she said, pointing down at the tracks.

"I know most of this country. And the back trails outlaws usually use to hide out. I'd like to reduce the odds by tracking

58

east and getting rid of those two before they catch a train all the way out of here."

The girl's face was flint. She stared eastward. "It's getting late. Can we stop talking now?"

L. P Quinn was glad to be shed of O'Clery and all the rest of them. Truth was, New York held no charm for him. Not anymore. But he sure as hell didn't want O'Clery or anyone else knowing his mind. *New York be damned,* he thought. There were a hundred places better than New York. All south from here. Denver was a roaring place. Or Dodge. *Hell,* he thought, *there was even Texas.* But if O'Clery was heading south to Cheyenne to catch the train, Quinn decided sitting tight for a couple of days might suit him just fine. Give O'Clery a couple of days to get wherever the hell he was going.

He thought about the Crow woman, and it sickened him a bit, even though he had taken part in the debasing of her. That had been the whisky. But when Burke finished her off with a bullet, it sobered him up. He hated Burke. Always had. Hated all of them. His idea from the start was just to get away. Dragging Tunneson to death? That was never part of what he wanted. Even while it was happening, Quinn had come close to putting a bullet in Burke's back. Killing those other two idiots, Byrnes and Murphy, would have been a pigeon shoot. It was that damn O'Clery. Quinn had actually put his hand on the butt of his pistol, but O'Clery was riding behind him, and that was never a good place to have him.

A wind was picking up, and L. P. Quinn stared into it. Across the flats a dust was coming up, turning loose a half dozen dust devils. *I've earned a rest,* he thought. Yonder was a thin grove of plane trees, so he nudged his horse in that direction. *A supper of grouse,* he thought. *Or whatever the hell crosses my gun sights.*

What Straw Dog saw bedeviled him—a man lying in the dust with a passel of coyote pups. This whole craziness was fifty yards away, so if he was ever to know who this animal-man was, he'd have to get closer. He was likely a loco, and nobody wanted to mix with that sort, fearful of a passing on of the madness. But madness was running high anyway. After leaving the fort, Straw Dog made a wide sweep toward the north, hoping to out flank the deserters, but it had proved a waste of time. Late last night he came upon the burnt trading post and tipi, and the buried bodies under the trees. When he saw the early evening breeze stirring Tunneson's neckerchief from the scrap of burnt wood, Straw Dog let out a cry of mourning. He had scouted with the sergeant for nigh eight snows.

Later, walking the mess of the destroyed yard, he puzzled over who else had been buried there. Likely all of Peacock's clan. And that would include the Crow woman, Turtle, who Tunneson loved. The tipi of the big buck, Bull Head, who was Peacock's chief horse breaker, might lie in the bigger grave. Probably with Peacock himself, his wife, and the Cheyenne girl. But who buried them? Not the deserters.

Now, as the pink sky turned scarlet, Straw Dog began putting things together. Was this strange coyote-man really the other horse breaker? Was this the young man they called Henry Mussel? The scent of coyote was strong, but the moon would soon be up, so he would wait until the mother left the den for the hunt. She knew he was there, squatting in the tall grass, but showed no fear. *Perhaps,* he thought, *our spirits are of one kind.*

After waiting a time the mother finally did leave the den, and Straw Dog edged closer, his eyes trained on the strange man. Likewise, Henry Mussel, still fighting with fever, watched as this dream-man crept nearer through the grass. The pups turned their eyes too, lowering their heads, soft growling burbling in their throats. Henry grunted something, and they fell silent. At ten feet, Straw Dog uttered a question in the native tongue and received a weak but clear affirmation.

Then the Indian scout spoke in the white man's tongue. "How bad are your wounds?"

"Bullet...remains. Fever."

"How did you get here?"

Henry rested his head against his arm. "I remember...*nothing*. Only...the rider."

"Your lodge still stands. I will get you there."

"How...far?"

"Not far. My horse is near."

There was just enough light from the small fire that Boone Crowe could see the girl's face. Their fixings were meager, but the salt pork that Crowe carried with him fried up quick in a pan, and later a brace of coffee brewed in a tin. He watched her, thinking about Little Feet again. So much had passed in his life since that time. More army. Then lawing. The woman he loved from when he was a boy in Pennsylvania, Eva, had come to a tragic end, not more than three years out. He had wanted her for his wife and sent for her by train from Nebraska.

These were painful remembrances. He found Eva's body at a place called Dead Woman Creek, named in her honor by the old Indian who had witnessed her death. After that, Crowe had given up all forms of happiness along those lines. Until he met Rose of Sharon. She had come into his life, set her love at his feet like a platter of riches, and he'd picked it up. But he feared now the thoughts she might have of him after today, were she to know. He had shot an unarmed man out of pure hatred. Out of cold blooded revenge.

The marshal in him would have made an arrest. Chained the bastard to his horse and paraded him back to the army for his

61

hanging. But he wasn't a marshal anymore. Just a man with a gun. He glanced at the girl again, and the vision of Willow Creek swallowed him, in all its dust, chaos, and fury. In the heat of battle, he had taken his pistol and put a bullet through the head of the captain. In the angry fury of the moment, he had murdered a murderer. And no one ever knew how the captain had died. So he thought. But this girl knew. This girl, Iron Hand, knew more about the darkness in his soul than his own wife did. Boone Crowe, the murderer.

He removed the piece of paper from his pocket that held the names of the deserters, and with the stub of pencil, he crossed off the names of Byrnes and Murphy, then stared at the remaining four names. If he had to, he would kill again.

"You are very quiet," the girl said.

He looked at her. "So are you."

The fire reflected in her eyes. "I never killed before. I have seen much killing. As a child. And these past hours ago. But never have I killed. I can no longer say that."

Boone returned the paper to his pocket. "I've seen more than my share too. But today… well, it was easy. Too easy."

She studied him. "Do you wish you had not killed that man?"

From another pocket he retrieved a half-smoked, leftover cigar, and after firing a twig, lit the cigar. He puffed, wondering how to answer her.

She watched him.

"Iron Hand," he said, speaking her name for the first time. "There are critters up in the mountains that generally keep to themselves. Bears and lions and such. It's only man who gets them disturbed. But mostly they leave folks alone." He stopped and took another puff, blowing out a blue trail of smoke. "These men…cowards I reckon…wanted no more part of the army. So they took to the hills. They could have found their freedom and figured that was enough. But they didn't."

Boone looked at his cigar, studying it, as if it might finish his speech for him. "You saw what they did. And…it was for no account. Except downright meanness. Peacock would have traded horses. He would have given them what they wanted, even at the point of a gun. But they killed my friend. They killed my friend's woman. And they killed your uncle and your aunt. They killed because they love killing. So, today..." He paused, drawing on the cigar again, his own eyes showing dark with bitterness. "These men are a plague. And I plan to rid the earth of them."

The girl seemed moved by his words. She had seen him as a child at Willow Creek, and she had seen him while they had done the burying. Even today, she had seen his rage in the town of Dog Run. But now, around this fire, she believed she might be seeing him for the very first time. She knew what the word *tormented* meant. She learned it at the Indian school and had applied it to herself. But this man, Boone Crowe, was even more tormented than she.

They cleaned up the salt pork and Boone, after snuffing out his cigar, finished off the coffee's bitter dregs. Finally he said, "We may find more of them soon, you know."

She nodded, then said, "I know."

He looked at her. "What was the white man's name they gave you at the Indian school?"

Her browed knitted. "Isabel."

He nodded. "I like that name," he said. "It suits you."

They heard a raven cawing in the distance, and they listened for a while. Finally Crowe said, "I need you to help identify these men. I need their faces. But...I don't want you doing any more killing." He looked into her eyes. "In the years ahead...it will be hard enough to forget the one today."

Chapter 8

IT WAS WELL PAST dark when the two Indians made it back to where the trading post once stood. Still feverish, Straw Dog helped Henry Mussel off of his horse and into the remaining tipi. He built a smoke fire, turning the interior into a sweat lodge, and set about examining the young man's wound. The bullet's entry point was just below the armpit on his right side and appeared to be lodged in the deep tissue of the back muscles.

But when he turned Henry over, he was surprised to see a swollen bulge on the left side of his back. The bullet had missed his spine, because his legs and arms worked, but appeared the slug had passed nearly all the way through and was just waiting to be cut out. So, counseling the young man on what he was about to do, he heated his knife blade and lanced the swollen bulge. With little effort the mushroomed slug pushed itself out. *Like a fat worm leaving the earth,* he thought.

Mussel had made no sound throughout this ordeal, which impressed Straw Dog, and the fever broke in the middle of the night, leaving the young man bathed in sweat. Straw Dog opened the tipi's smoke flaps and cleared the air inside. Through the opening he could see that the sun was making its appearance, throwing a flush of color across the prairie. But the night had been long. He would try and find his own sleep now.

But for a long time he lay awake, thinking about the deserters and how it would be very hard now to track them. He wondered again who might have buried the sergeant and the others. Searching his memory, he suddenly found himself fully awake. He sat up. After listening to the coward Gillespie, he had remounted his horse and left the fort directly. He had been filled with a bull's rage over Gillespie's refusal to send help. And he knew to stay would be the death of the captain. And now, knowing that his friend was dead, he knew what he must do.

This captain would meet a death. Not like that of Fetterman. Not like that of Custer. Not for his stupidity. They had died because their hearts were too puffed up. They thought they could never die. But Gillespie would die for his dishonor. But this is not what had shot Straw Dog up out of his near sleep. It was the now remembered figure of the man who was called *crow*. Just as he had been riding away from the fort, he saw this crow-man atop his pale horse, riding into the fort. He had heard the sergeant talk of this man. And he had seen him two times or more. There was no mistaking now. It was this crow-man who buried his friend.

Straw Dog sat, looking at the fading fire. He remembered the tales the sergeant told of this tall old man. Long ago, in the desert. Against the Apaches. He smiled, trying once again to see this crow-man, as he rode into the fort. He laid back down on his blanket. Now he knew—there would be no rest for the bad men.

O'Clery rode through the night, wanting to reach the railhead in Cheyenne in another day. But he and his horse were both wasted, and so he stopped, just as the sun broke over the low, flat horizon. There was water here, but it was bitter, and so the horse refused to drink. He pulled off the saddle, checked the ground for unwanted visitors, threw down a bedroll and was asleep in minutes.

A wind rose up while O'Clery slept, but he lay undisturbed in the shade of a bank of bushes. But on the wind the horse picked up the scent of fresher water. It filled its nostrils with want. So, following its horse sense, it lowered its head to the sand and began a slow trek in the direction of the wind, every now and then stopping to breath in the sweet aroma, while seeking the source of the water. By the time he woke, hours later, O'Clery was stunned to realize he was horseless. Like a lost child, he stumbled up and down the surrounding hills, trying to find the animal, but by then the wind had erased the tracks into a high plains folly of nothingness.

Further, O'Clery's wandering had disoriented him to the point that he couldn't even find his way back to his camp. So now he was without horse, water, food, or saddle. He stared into the sky, at the midday sun. It was directly over him, so he couldn't even determine east from west. And he was heading south. The only possession he had now was his army issue revolver. He pulled it from its holster and blew the sand off of it. His belt carried three cartridges, but the pistol itself had only three more, so he fully loaded the pistol. He would have to wait an hour at least to judge properly the direction of the sun's decent. From that he would determine which way was south, a quarter angle off west. And then he would start heading that way. On foot.

L. P. Quinn was inclined to wait another day, not wishing to encounter O'Clery for any reason again. It wasn't that he was afraid of him; it was just that he was free now and had no preference toward seeing any of those wasters again. Besides, he was still working out his own plans, and that was done best at rest, with a mind clear of distraction. He would need to make some kind of living, and for a while anyway, it might even have to be an honest living. Back in New York he had worked in a butcher's shop, his uncle's, same as Burke had. Surely, if the town was big enough, he might find some work along those lines. He had no skill at gambling with cards, but he could read some, and that was always something he might lean on.

He had idled away the morning, and now, stirring the fire up again, he heated the last can of beans he'd grabbed as an afterthought from Peacock's shelves. At the time, eating was far off in his thinking. What he wanted now was meat, and all through the morning he had heard the cackling and chatter of game birds. He would attend to that closer to dusk when the birds were feeding. Quinn knew he'd have to conserve his ammunition.

It was a good hour later when he heard the sound of approaching hoof beats. They were coming from a distance yet, moving slow but strangely deliberate, and he gauged them to be from the west. *Of all the damn luck,* he thought. Looking around, he searched his camp for anything that might reveal his identity. His recent history. His carbine was army issue, a thing he foolishly kept. But nothing else. Whoever this was, he'd explain that away in a hurry.

Hell, he thought. *It might even be O'Clery, come back. Or Burke. If it's that damn kid, I'll just kill him outright.*

The land was too flat to hide, his camp being in the belly of a small swell. If this rider was coming straight on, he'd be easy to stumble on. He'd just have to play it smart. He took the carbine and laid it by his saddle, then covered it with his bedroll. If this stranger looked like trouble, he'd use his pistol. It was a more common Colt. Near every man in the territory had one similar.

Quinn turned finally, pushed back the brim of his hat and faced the direction of the approaching horseman, as if chairman of a welcoming committee. He squinted and saw an old man with sweat-banded hat and a long face of gray whiskers. The horse, as it came on, was near invisible, so light in color, not white, just plain colorless. Looking back at the man, he saw little threat, just an old, worn down drifter, or aged cowpuncher. He stood, waiting for the stranger to close in, and then he put on his best, broad smile.

The man on the pale horse pulled up, nodding a greeting. They looked at each other for a moment more, then the rider said, "I saw yer smoke. Was hopin I might borrow it for some coffee. I got the makings."

Quinn studied the man, then said, "Coffee? Why, shore. If you be willin to share yer grinds, I'll be pleased ta' share me flames. Step down." In his mind he believed this was the best way to rid himself of this fellow. Let the old boy coffee up, then he'll move on. "Let me give the fire a stir."

Boone Crowe stepped down from his Ghost Horse, letting the reins hang loose. He watched the man tending to the fire, then scanned the far side of the swell, looking to see if the girl was close. They had seen the cook fire's smoke a long ways off and had left their horses hidden in a draw and crept to the hilltop. Crowe was rarely without his officer's telescope that he'd carried since the States War. Iron Hand had never looked through one before, so he extended it and let her peer into it. It took her a while before she found the smoke and its source. When she finally found it, she stiffened.

Whaddya see? he'd asked, taking the glass from her. He could make out the man, moving around a smoky cook fire. *Recognize him?*

She took the glass again and looked hard and long. Finally, handing it back, she nodded firmly. *Quinn.*

How'd you know?

Hair. It is red. Very red.

There's more than a heap of redheaded men in the world.

She had flashed him a scornful look. Her words came tight. *He wears Uncle Pea's hat. And the horse. It is one of those from the corral.*

That had settled it. But when he'd told her that he was going in alone, and that she had to stay put, it angered her further. *Look,* he'd said. *You've done your part. If I need you, I'll holler. Just don't show yerself.*

Now Boone was playing the jolly old drifter. He took in what he could while this man, Quinn, toyed with his fire. Not much for belongings—a saddle, blanket, and the clothes on his back. And what Iron Hand said was a stolen hat, black with a broad brim. It might well be true, but after yesterday's violence, he wanted to be sure. He'd play it cool, not wanting another murder on his conscience.

"What brings ye through this desolate place?" Quinn asked with strained cheerfulness.

"Horses," Crowe answered.

"That be a fact. There 'pears to be plenty about."

Crowe didn't want to drag this thing out, so he decided to press to the point. "Wild horses, to be a fact. I'm headin to Fort Laramie to partner up with my old friend."

Quinn stood still for a long moment. The mention of the fort had turned a knob on his easiness, but he said nothing.

"Goin to fetch us a batch for the army down there. They'll keep what's good and auction off what's not."

Still Quinn said nothing.

"There's always that trading post too. Old man Peacock deals in horses. So I've heard anyway. You know him?"

"No," Quinn said, too quickly, his single word like a bitten-off carrot.

Crowe was ready for the harbinger. "Maybe you know my friend then. Sergeant Tunneson. Lancelot Tunneson."

This time Quinn stiffened visibly. He turned then, facing Crowe, his feinted effort at pleasantry vanished. "What you want, mister? It ain't coffee, I'm feelin."

It was Boone Crowe's turn to be silent. But his gaze was like an awl, piercing the other man's endurance. Very slowly he eased his gun holster forward onto his right hip, casual like.

"Are you here to rob me?" Quinn said, a challenge, not a question.

"I'm here to take you back to Fort Laramie. So's you can hang."

All pretense was gone now, and Crowe saw the true nature of Quinn, the cold, violent sneer of blood and confidence. "The hell ye say."

"You know what for too, don't ya?"

"I don't."

"You're wearing Peacock's hat. And yer ridin one of his bay horses."

L. P. Quinn was a lot of things, a two-bit thief, a conman, and deadly with a knife. But he was not a notable gunman. Yet, this man before him was older, shabby, and saddle worn. And Quinn, by his nature, had a lust for blood; it had been born into him. So the prospect of violence was something too strong to resist. He made a mad grab for his pistol.

Crowe's ugly old Army Colt was up, and the loud bark of it was deafening. Quinn's pistol had barely cleared the holster when Crowe's bullet drove him backward. He landed on his backside in the dust, and he just sat there, a sprout of red on his chest. He still held his own pistol, but in the moment of instant shock, he'd forgotten about it. The old marshal moved forward and kicked it out of the dying man's hand.

"Do you know yer crimes, Quinn?"

The deserter looked up through glassy eyes, then nodded his red head. He was still sitting up, but the bullet had made a big hole, and he was bleeding heavily.

"Where's the rest of them? We already got Byrnes. And Murphy."

Dying as he was, this news seemed to surprise Quinn. He tried to digest it, but his breathing was becoming shallow. Still, he managed a gasp. "Watch...yer step...with that *bastard*...O... O'Clery."

"Where's he?"

"Yon-der...south. Chey..." It was the last of him. Quinn never did fall over, just died sitting there, hat off, a flick of red hair being licked by the wind.

Iron Hand rode up a few minutes later. She dismounted, looked at Crowe only briefly, then walked to Quinn and spit on him. Dead as he was, she spit, and then spit again.

Baby Sullivan was a mess. All his bravado had been stripped away by the wind, the hunger, the thirst, and the aloneness. But mostly by the black root of indecision that had started growing like a thorn inside him and now had taken over. He'd even cried around his dry camp the night before. Real tears, those of a true baby. He'd looked around for someone to hang the blame on, but it was only himself who was here to share the cold, frightful night with.

His so-called glory over killing an Indian had already worn off, as had the violent, heaving release his loins had felt with the

Indian woman. She had already been used up by the time he got to her. That glory, if it was such, lay like a sickness on him now. If anyone deserved being killed, it was that damn Burke. He was the one. Claimed to have it all figured out.

Baby sat on his horse and stared off to where the mountains of Laramie rose pretty in the distance. But he did not see pretty, only loneliness. Only more fear. He didn't even know what day it was, or even the proper month, if he thought hard enough. He just never cared about such notions, only the next meal, be it from his uncle's table in New York, or his next bean and gravy slop dished up by the army. Hell, he didn't even have a proper grasp on how old he was. He'd just always been Baby.

In the far grass he saw the pointy horns of antelope, their curious heads watching back at him and their white tails as they turned away. Closer, in the near fallings of a tree, he saw blackbirds, a dozen or more, quarreling over berry and bug. *How was it*, he wondered, *that they knew all about who and what they were, and they only had a brain the size of a pea?* And yet here he was, dumb and scared and no place to find an answer.

He punched himself hard on his thigh. "Wake up, ye damn fool!" he shouted. "Figure out some damn things." He wondered where the others were, not that he cared that much. O'Clery had pretended to like him, till he saw it was just a mean joke. What he should have done was ride with Pup and Byrnes. Byrnes especially never spoke a word against him. And Pup was just Pup. *Wonder where they be?* he thought.

He climbed down from his horse and the blackbirds scattered. It can't be that hard, he reasoned. First things first, maybe. Old Sarge used to say that. But then the image of Tunneson, leaning against a fence post with a lance driven through him put a sourness to his thoughts. Seems old Sarge got the order backward. Last things first. Dying before living.

Chapter 9

They had two horses in tow now, the one from Dog Run that Byrnes had ridden, and now the bay that Quinn had stolen. The girl reclaimed her uncle's hat, and she wore it now out of pure remembrance, Crowe guessed. She found the carbine Quinn had hidden under his bedroll, and the pistol that was not fast enough out of his holster to give him more years of life. They did not bury him, nor did they even lay him on his back, only left him sitting upright for the curious coyotes or wolves to feast on. He deserved no better.

Iron Hand was few on words, but her mood seemed to cheer in a grisly sort of way. She had witnessed horrors at the hands of these men, and she was realizing a degree of satisfaction in seeing them put to justice. A bad and ugly justice, Crowe had told her, if justice it was at all. Crowe had never liked the killing, but he was no stranger to it. He still carried the ghastly picture of Lancelot Tunneson in his mind, and he hoped that it would stay there until the killing was done. After that, he hoped it would go away and never haunt him again. But he was not that foolish.

They were heading south, in the hope that Quinn had not given them a bum lead. Crowe had scratched the killer's name off of the list, leaving only Baby Sullivan, Cletus Burke, and Finn O'Clery. "You know," Crowe said, "luck's been with us. And not with them. But luck changes. I hope yer in for a long ride."

The girl grunted. "I have no place to go. Only where their trail goes."

"And I wish there was a trail. But there ain't. Just a direction. But," he took off his hat and shielded his eyes, "I've been on this track a' heap of times. All the way to Cheyenne. If this O'Clery is there, or gettin there, we'll find him." He gazed around him, at the open country. "What markings does he have that we might recognize him?"

"I will know him for his evil look."

"That won't do. What else?"

The girl breathed deep. "Through the crack of my hiding place, I saw his face. I was frightened. He came so close to the wall I was hiding behind. A secret place Uncle Pea had made. For other reasons. But he put me in there. Do not move, he told me. Never, for anything." Her voice grew thin, and she waited for several moments before continuing. "This one. O'Clery. He came and stared at the wall I was behind. I thought he saw me through the crack. But he was only looking at something else. But he laughed. Loud and awful. And when he did this I saw that he had missing teeth. In the front. He is very thin. And his ugly face made him look like a laughing dead man."

Crowe nodded. "That'll do."

They rode with the Laramie Mountains to their right, not that far off, the slanting hills, slopping gradually into the sharper teeth of peaks. It was a country that, apart from the wickedness of men, was a place to love. And Boone Crowe loved it. The Pennsylvania farm he left to fight the Johnny Rebs for was tolerable pretty, but even then it was getting crowded. And the places of cannon and smoke in the valleys of the Shenandoah was so spilled with blood that for the time he was there the beauty had been taken from it. But this territory of Wyoming was near the same kind of love a man could have for a woman.

"Are you having one of your daydreams?"

Crowe looked at the girl. "It shows that easy, does it?"

"It shows," she said, the faintest smile tightening her lips.

"The land's done no harm to me. Oh, it may have tried a time or two. But not out of meanness."

"Do you have a wife, Boone Crowe?"

"I do," he said. "A good one that I don't deserve."

Her smile widened. Then her expression turned more sober. "I think you are a man with many ghosts."

Crowe considered that. "It shows that easy, does it?" he repeated.

"It shows," she said again.

He stared straight ahead, wondering what else this girl might think of him. "I reckon I've got my share. They're hard to get rid of. They know me too good. They've figured me for an easy mark. Some kind of sucker for regret."

The girl edged her horse closer to his, and without reason or explanation, she reached out and touched his arm. The gesture lasted but a moment, and beyond a brief second when their eyes met, it was over. But Crowe felt her touch for many hours and many days afterward. It meant something that words could never convey, that even years in the searching of meanings in the big books of knowledge, it could never be known. But it was known between them, and that was all that mattered.

One precious item had not run off with Finn O'Clery's horse, and that was a bottle of rye whisky he'd pilfered at the trading post, one he'd even managed to secret from the rest of the gang. It was approaching noon now, the sun putting a direct fire down upon his uncovered head. Uncovered because he'd managed to lose his hat while stumbling drunkenly in search of his lost horse. He held the bottle by the long neck and stood protesting against the wind. "Ye'll not fetch me," he howled. But it was not the wind he railed against. For hours he had been addressing his dead father, Hatchet John O'Clery, deadliest man in all of Five Points.

O'Clery stumbled again and found himself on his backside. He pointed the bottle accusingly at the specter of his father. "Ye'll not drag me to that bloody ground."

Who's to avenge me, Finn, me boy? If not ye?

The drunken deserter uttered an oath, then said, "Paid up yer own debt, did ye not? To even up the score. I've got me own devils doggin me." True it was, as a fifteen-year-old Irish boy in the murky violence of Five Points, where starvation, disease, and battling gangs were all in the daily diet. His own mother had been clubbed to death one night, picking the wrong alley to cross down.

True. Ye have a gift for it.

"I'm free of it now…you noisy old devil." He took another drink, then measured its contents against the sun. "After you got yer due…why…I figured I'd be next. Sins o' the father. All that. They…they was on to me."

There was some days. Afore all that. When I was a fresh lad meself. Me and me brothers would play at the Fresh Pond. Ice skate on the Collect. Till folks started dumpin dead horses in it. Turned to rot. But them was the days. You 'member yer uncles, don't ye?

O'Clery searched for something to throw at his father's image but found only loose clods of dirt. "Shut up, old man." He lay down finally and stood the bottle on the ground beside him. He was twelve when he took a cudgel to a man's head, killing him. It was for his purse. He gave the few recovered coins to his mother and felt himself a successful breadwinner. It never stopped. His fear grew, though. Years later, a mob killed his father, leaving him butchered like a chicken where the whole of Five Points would find him the next morning. A blood oath carried out.

The army was signing men up to tame the savages, so he left for the frontier. And now, here he was, drunk on his back, no horse, nothing to eat, and that damned old father of his, babbling to no good end.

Straw Dog knew well the big man, the soldier named Burke. He remembered how that man looked at Tunneson whenever the sergeant's back was turned. It was a look he knew well, for it was the same look given him when called a red savage. On patrols, this man Burke always gave his eyes to the women at this trading camp.

Tunneson would bring a small troop with him when keeping a lookout for troublesome Utes who might come north. Straw Dogs' own people, the Snake, or Shoshone as some have called them, were scattered through this territory and the next. There was no love between them and the Sioux or Northern Cheyenne. But now all Indians were either tamed or hunted. Many even dead. These times had brought many of them together. Peacock's wife was Cheyenne. The woman whom Tunneson loved was a Crow. Crows and Cheyenne were bitter enemies, but Peacock hated no Indian.

There was a girl once too, Straw Dog thought. *Peacock always keep her hidden when the soldiers came. But I saw her.*

She was probably dead too. Along with the others. So he gave her no further thought.

While Henry Mussel slept, Straw Dog left the tipi and walked to the copse of trees where his old friend was buried. Tunneson had picked him from a group of other Snakes, braves who had lived this country and knew it. The sergeant paced in front of the assembly, eyeing each one with a soldier's sharp eye. He asked them questions. Questions that he knew the answers to but hoped to find those Indians who also knew the answers. Questions about the land, and the seasons, and where enemies might hide. And tracking questions. After a long time, Tunneson put his hand on Straw Dog's shoulder and told him to come. They had ridden together ever since.

And now his old friend was dead.

He remembered the look on Captain Gillespie's face when he asked for soldiers to help find Tunneson. The captain gave a laugh like the grunt of a mule. He said, *I have problems of my own. Tunneson can work things out for himself.* Straw Dog, after remembering this, placed an open palm on the top of the dirt mound that held his friend.

"This hand," he said, "it will avenge you."

Cletus Burke rode slowly, saving his horse. It was a black from Peacock's corral of broke stock, and it was a good one. He wanted to preserve it for the long trek he had before him. It was weeks away from serious bad weather, and even if he hit the mountains soon, it would still be easy traveling. He had never been this far west, or this far north, even though there was a good bit of north left to see. Montana was making some noise, what with copper and silver strikes, and if he played it safe, he might be able to cash in.

Burke's thoughts were mostly on the miles ahead, and the different places they would take him. It was not his wish to do a lot of mingling. He'd passed a few lonesome homesteads, some even with folks out in the fields, or working around their simple homes. But he'd turned off, moving away. Not because he feared anything by their presence, rather a simple desire to be left alone. Alone with his own thoughts and not having to parley about with other people's thoughts. For the first time as long as he could remember, he was alone, and it suited him plenty.

He thought about the kid once or twice, wondering how deep his regret was by striking out alone. Damn fool, kid. Didn't have the brains of a cornstalk. His wild fever to kill himself an Indian likely wore off by now. But it was a catching fever. *We all got it then,* he thought. It was like an explosion. First dragging Tunneson. Getting to the trading post and seeing that Peacock and his missus was already killed by that fool kid. *It seemed to knock the whole wide world off its hinges,* he thought.

It was the woman, though. That came first from need. And then from hatred. Hatred for her, being a redskin. And mostly for Tunneson, because she was his woman. That was plain to see from the times they stopped there. *Lookin for Utes? Hell,* he thought, *lookin for her, he was.* Couldn't blame him, though. She was a prize of a woman. Indian or no.

Burke watched the land. Over another rise he spied yet one more farm, where a lone man followed behind a mule-pulled plow. *Why do they keep doin it?* he wondered. He knew nothing of farming, except it never gave back much. Hard work and then the grave. *Leavin a broke-down wife and a clutch of young-uns.* He felt pity for the man at the plow. If he had already struck his vein, he'd gladly toss the man a handful. *Buy yer woman a dress, ya fool. Or sell out and take up with the world.*

But he hadn't struck his vein yet, so he rode on past. But the woman did not leave his thoughts. Not just this farmer's woman but any woman. He was himself surprised that he hadn't been written off already by some diseased whore, since those were the only women he'd ever known. Likely this farm wife was plain as a fence post. But ahead, he hoped, he might fool some respectable woman into thinking he himself was respectable. Ahead the sun was turning the color of gold, the same color of the riches he sought. But it was also the gold of a girl's hair he saw once. So long ago, in a life removed from memory, all most. An escaped life.

Eleonora. That was her name, he remembered. It wasn't really her name; it was just the name he had attached to her. In his imagination. He'd seen her at a train station the day he was shipped out west to join his regiment. A soldier among soldiers. In uniform. Her look toward him was so quick it was hardly a look at all. But seeing her full-faced, her hair well-tended and the yellow of fresh buttercups, filled his nights with a pain deeper than a wound.

Eleonora, in his dreams she became to him. Ever after.

Night was falling and Boone Crowe and Iron Hand fretted some over the lack of signs. In the late afternoon they had come across a pair of cowpunchers pushing a dozen yearlings in an easterly direction. The one riding drag stopped long enough to tip his hat. "Seen a lone rider out here?" Crowe asked. "Rail thin fella with a mouth of missing teeth."

"Ain't seen nuthin but trail dust and these critter's backsides," he answered cheerfully.

"Nobody?"

"Nope. Surprised I seen you, fer all this blamed dust."

79

Boone did notice, though, that the cowboy's eyes weren't so full of dirt that he didn't keep a steady gaze on the girl.

So, they wondered, had Quinn, in his dying breath, led them astray. It was too early to give up on O'Clery. If he was headed for Cheyenne, they had nothing to do but keep going. But no more tonight. It was time to make camp. The horses were feeling the trail hours too. They would leave early in the morning.

Less than five miles farther south, a prairie dog crept ever closer to the whisky-wasted body of Finn O'Clery, curious to the point of daring. The critter sniffed the strong sent of alcohol, and his head sprang back in annoyance. The man was alive, and a steady stream of snores made his loose lips tremble as in a spasm. The animal shoved its nose in the man's neck but got only a slurred moan in reply. *Shtop it...Betty.*

Chapter 10

BACK IN BUFFALO, MARSHAL Rud Lacrosse was just returning from investigating a complaint of a stolen cow from old Dabner Wilcox. Turned out the cow had not been rustled at all, only stuck in a mud hole and desperate to get unstuck. So, with rope and ginger maneuvering, Rud and Dabner managed to rescue the desperate beast. But now, riding back into town, Rud could see Judge Schaffer standing on the boardwalk in front of the courthouse, waving at him.

"Where's Crowe?" the Judge hollered, even before Lacrosse could rein in.

The Judge was a hard one to ignore, and by the look on his flushed face, this was not going to be a pleasant visit. "I've just come from his ranch," he said. "For the second time. Ain't a soul there but that old Rufus."

"He isn't there because he isn't there, Judge. Rose is gone back east, and Boone's off chasing wild horses for the army."

"Wild horses? The army? What in blazes is he doing that for?"

Lacrosse had not dismounted, and so he looked down at the Judge and shrugged. "Anyone's guess, sir."

"Well, when'll he be back?"

The young marshal looked up the street toward the telegraph office. Stanley motioned for him to come on. *What the heck does he want now?* Rud thought.

The Judge was still talking. "Fine. He picked a fine time to be gone."

Lacrosse was losing interest in the Judge and getting more interested in Stanley, who was still waving at him.

"I want to talk to him the minute he gets back to town. You tell him that."

"Yes sir. I will."

Neither spoke for a moment. Finally, Lacrosse said, "Anything else, your Honor?"

By now Judge Schaffer was already lost in new thoughts. He

shook his head absently, and the marshal used this as an excuse to nudge his horse in the direction of Stanley, who had finally returned to his office. Hoping the Judge wouldn't think of something else, Lacrosse made a hasty retreat. Once at the telegraph office, he slid from his saddle and stepped inside.

"Telegraph, Rud," Stanley said.

"For me?"

"All the way from Baltimore."

Rud Lacrosse, a one-time academic from the east, schooled in the sciences, had fled to the west to seek adventure. Finding himself under the tutelage of Boone Crowe, adventure he had found, to the very office he now held, that of United States Marshal for Wyoming Territory, Crowe's old job. He looked at Stanley, and then at the telegraph, which was being held out to him. *Bad news always comes by telegraph,* he thought.

Stanley wiggled the yellow paper impatiently. "It ain't no snake, Rud. It won't bite."

"It might," he said, taking hold of it but not looking at it. "Mind if I sit down?"

Pointing at his desk and the chair behind it, Stanley nodded.

Sitting, Lacrosse finally spread the telegram out on the desk in front of him, flattening it with his palm, and read. Again he read it. Twice more. Then he looked at Stanley, who obviously knew its contents. "When did you get this?"

"Jist now. Right when I saw you comin up the street."

"It wants a reply."

"Of course it does."

"But..."

"It don't say when. You might want to think on it."

Rud nodded, his mind swirling. "Paige. I'll have to...she'll want to..."

"Yer wife. Sure. She'll help you decide. They always do."

82

"Redemption," Baby Sullivan cried, his voice pitching up like a bird's. It was a big word for his little head, but he'd heard it before, so he knew its meaning. Ahead, a mile off where the low hills of the Laramie range butted together, was a town. A small town, but a town just the same. There'll be people there. He tried to remember if he had a single cent to his name. *Hell*, he thought. *I'll work for a meal. Or steal. Makes no mind to me.* He nudged his horse into a trot, making a beeline for the single dusty street that divided six weather-beaten buildings. "Redemption," he said again.

Arriving, he dismounted in time to see a big tumbleweed fight for space in the middle of the street, blowing and rolling in the same direction from which he'd come. A pair of locals, sitting on a bench, taking turns spitting brown tobacco juice into the street, gave him a fair-minded glance. "Howdy," one of them said.

Baby felt overjoyed to hear a human voice. He nodded a happy reply. He searched his pockets and came up with a folded dollar and a two-bit piece, given to him by Burke, who had robbed the cigar box Peacock had kept his money in. Baby looked at the man who had spoken. "Food," he said.

The two old timers continued to spit. Finally, after a shared wink, one of them said, "Vittles it's yer after, is it?"

Baby nodded. "I'm plum wasted for hunger."

"Well, ya wandered into the right place," the old man said, a shade of undetected mockery in his voice. "Darling Annie, she does the cookin fer the whole town." He spit. "S'long as ya likes beans."

"I'll eat beans," Baby nearly howled. "I'll eat anything."

The old man who had not spoken was beginning to giggle.

"That there's a good oath," said the first. "Account of she throws whatever she can find right there in the pot."

Baby Sullivan's worn out boots shuffled anxiously in the dusty street. "I'm obliged. Where can she be found? This, Annie?"

"Darling Annie," the old man corrected. "Right there," he said, pointing a crooked finger toward a red-painted door across the street. "She'll fetch ya what ya need."

Tying his horse to the rail, Baby made haste toward the red door. What he found inside the dark interior, besides the mixed aroma of body sweat, pig leavings, and a straw-strewn floor, was a woman the size of a full grown bear. Even in the dim light he could see her narrow, black eyes staring at him from under a witch's wiry tangle of hair that stood atop her head like a tumbleweed. Her dress, if that's what it was, was little more than a blanket with a hole cut for her head and arm openings. She moved like a mountain, and Baby watched as she planted a boulder-sized fist where her hip had once been, now just more of the mountain.

But when she spoke, her voice was velvety as a pigeon's coo. "Hello, sonny."

Baby could feel his Adam's apple tighten as he struggled to swallow. "Ahhh…"

"Are you hungry, little man?"

"So…some…me reckons."

"Well, you look like someone squeezed the last vitamin right out of you."

Baby had no idea what a vitamin was, so he just stood there, the smell of the place starting to work on his eyes.

Darling Annie pointed to the corner of the room with a finger swelled like a sausage. "Find that chair and sit. I'll bring you some stew."

"Stew?"

Neither her voice, nor her laugh, now delivered, had any business being attached to her body. With eyes closed she could be a sweet farmer's daughter. "You talk like a little Irish lad. So, let's name it Irish stew. Just for you, baby."

Baby, he thought. *How'd she know my name?*

He found the chair and sat waiting, and he heard her approach before he saw her, the straw-covered floor planks moaning their grief under her weight. Reaching out with hairy arms, she placed a huge wooden bowl in front of him, a spoon lodged in the middle of its steaming, brown gum. The aroma that drifted up from it seemed tolerable, considering all the other smells in the room. Baby's stomach gave a roar from deep down, so lifting the spoon, he braved a bite. It rested on his tongue for a moment, allowing him to judge its texture. Sure enough, there were beans in there. And meat too. The old man hadn't lied. So he swallowed.

Remembering his hunger, Baby threw caution to the wind and began eating in earnest.

"You like it," she said, that sweet voice again. Baby thought it might could be the voice of his very own mother, if he'd ever had one. None that he ever knew anyway. He sucked on the beans and chewed on the meat and nodded his head in silent appraisal. After he had finished, Darling Annie brought him a tin can with two-fingers of corn whisky. "Here's to settle it in," she cooed.

Baby sniffed at the tin can's contents, then lifting it to his lips, swallowed it in one gulp. It was the last thing he remembered.

Iron Hand saw the horse and recognized it immediately. She had risen at first light, following the creek they had camped by so she could wash her face and fill the canteens. The gelding, which had abandoned Finn O'Clery for this fresh stream the day before, stood partially hidden behind an olive tree. It had been unburdened of its saddle, but its bit and reins still hung loose. Seeing the girl, the horse came to her without being beckoned, her familiar scent from her days riding it.

"Look at you," the girl said softly. She said this without letting her eyes search the surroundings. Where the horse was, so would O'Clery be. Taking up the reins, she led it back to the camp.

Boone Crowe grasped the entire scene when he saw her approaching. "Did you see him?"

She shook her head. "Too dark. He might be there. Somewhere. I just wanted to get the horse and get away." She held up the canteens. "I didn't fill them."

"It'll keep." Boone pulled his Colt and checked the cylinder. "I need to make a search. Stay here."

"Always you tell me that," she said, angrily.

He ignored her. "I won't be long. If you hear gunshots, bring the Henry. But dammit. Don't be shooting until you know who yer shootin at."

She turned her back on him, but he had already started walking to the creek and to the trees where she'd found the horse.

Crowe was gone for a quarter of an hour, but during that time not a sound was heard, besides birdsong and the occasional banter of a raven. When he finally did return to the camp, his pistol had been holstered and he wore a look of puzzlement. "Nothing," he said. "No human sign at all. Just hoof prints and horse apples. If this was O'Clery's horse, it ain't anymore."

She looked at him, searching his face for an answer. "What?"

"Yer sure that's Peacock's horse."

"Do not ask me that again."

"I jist have to be sure."

She gathered up the canteens for a second time and tromped back down to the creek.

Boone Crowe shook his head. *Women,* he thought.

Later, they added the gelding to the string of gathered horses and continued on. They had to settle for a cold breakfast of jerky and no coffee, which cemented both into grumpy moods. Crowe tried to put together in his mind the possibilities of why the horse was without the rider. Had O'Clery fallen off? Or died somehow? Had Straw Dog found him first and killed him? Or was Straw Dog even in the vicinity? The one thing he did know was that Quinn had not lied. Somewhere, O'Clery either *was*, or *is*.

"Maybe he is dead," the girl said.

"I was just thinking that."

"I hope he is not. I want to see him die."

Crowe had a lot he wanted to say about that but kept quiet. After a long while he said, "Tell me about the Indian school."

"Why do you want to know about that?"

"It'll tell me more about you."

"Why do you want to know more about me?"

"I have my reasons."

The girl's expression darkened. "We were taken by train. They cut our hair. They made the boys wear white man's clothes. No more horses. Pencils. Papers. Books. We were punished if we spoke Lakota. I ran away. Three times. There is nothing more to say."

"How long were you there?"

"Too long."

Boone turned the Ghost Horse in front of her so she had to stop. He looked at her. "Listen to me. I knew all that. I've heard all those stories many times. And they don't make me happy. But I'm poor at makin talk, so the best I can say is, I want for you a happy life. I want for you to grow out of your sorrow."

She knitted her eyebrows, confused by this strange talk.

"I ain't trying to change you. But…I was once in love with a girl like you."

Iron Hand looked surprised. "A Cheyenne?"

He nodded. "A long time ago. It was years before Willow Creek."

Her eyes were wide now. "What happened to her?"

"She was sent away. To Florida. On a train. Jist like you."

"You could not stop them?"

"I was away when they did it." Even now, talking about it was painful.

Neither spoke for a while, each sitting on their saddles, gathering their thoughts. Finally Boone went on. "I have spent a lot of time these past days. Thinking. Wondering about the hate we're both carryin around. It's poison, Isabel. And it will grow if not attended to."

She was startled by his use of her white man's name. But it sounded different coming from his mouth. It was not hurtful like it had been when forced upon her.

"I'm over fifty years old. A life of memories. The things I am going to do. The things I have already done—they are all tied up with those memories. I'm old and I'm hard. But you…" He was struggling now. He'd hardly ever spoken so tenderly to anyone, besides Rose. And even that was difficult sometimes. "Dammit, girl. Let me jist get this out. You are a fine…a beautiful young woman. I want you to live past your anger. Past your hatred. I don't want it to…to poison you. I want for you a happy life," he said again, his voice filled with emotion. "You are right. I do have many ghosts. If you can…let go of yours."

Chapter 11

THERE WAS PAIN IN Finn O'Clery's head, and when he woke from his drunken stupor, he was surprised to find that there was no Injun tomahawk splitting open his skull, only the daggers of a terrible hangover. The sun had a hot hand on his face, and he growled with savage anger at it. Rolling onto his side, he reached for his pistol, so as to shoot the light of it out, but discovered his holster was empty. Here lay another mystery to his unthinking mind. Where was his Colt? Where was his horse? Where was his knife? His hand swept the back of his belt—the knife was still there, sheathed.

For the first time in a long time the smell of his own unwashed body repulsed him. Sweat on top of sweat. His shirt had become stiff with the salty stuff and he reeked. Sitting up, the pain in his head nearly forced him back down, so he put his head between his knees and shuddered out a string of uneven dog-like pants. Five minutes later he was swaying on wobbly legs. Then he remembered the bad water. And how his horse had wanted no part of it.

Like the day before, O'Clery began another aimless search for his belongings. Two brushy, low hummocks away he saw where his camp had been, nothing there but the hole he had pawed in the sand where he sat, adding up his misery. The bitter buffalo wallow was close by, where it had always been, a sickly green pond beneath a cluster of closely knotted saplings. He staggered toward it, and upon reaching it, fell to his knees and stared into its muck. Carelessly he lifted up several palmfuls and splashed it on his face. It stunk worse than he did, but he next removed his shirt and splashed more water on his chest and arms.

Looking around, he eyed the cluster of trees and decided that the shade they offered from the hot sun might be the very cure for his hangover. He circled the wallow and stood beneath the cool, welcoming dimness. There was a patch of struggling grass too, so without a second thought, he stretched out upon it and tried to wish away his headache. A confused bird was chirping a mixed-up song, and within a minute, Finn O'Clery was asleep.

As they rode south, Boone Crowe kept a vigilant eye open for game. The range they were passing through, he knew, was a region of unpopulated wilderness. Another Dog Run would be a welcome sight, but he knew of no towns in this lonely place. Before they camped this night, they would need some real food. The saddlebags on O'Clery's captured horse held scant more than the same jerked meat they already had. He thought about Rose of Sharon, and the eggs and potatoes she would have put before him if he were home now. If *she* were home now.

He'd seen a number of antelope on the grazing slopes, but he knew his Henry, as good a rifle as it was, did not win any long-distance prizes. He would have to get closer, which he would have to do alone. Nudging the Ghost Horse alongside the girl he suggested they stop. "This here is barren country," he said. "If we expect to have fresh meat by tonight, I'm going to have to do a hunt."

Iron Hand looked at him, waiting for the rest of it.

"Over that next rise," he went on, pointing. "You can tend to the horses. I doubt they'll wander off. There's a bit of grass, and they've had water. Tie 'em to a clump of sagebrush if you're not sure."

"A gun," she said.

He looked at her for a long moment, then nodded. Reaching into his saddle bag, he retrieved a small, birds eye .38 caliber pistol. He checked the cylinder and then handed it to her. "It's got four rounds in it. If you run into trouble, fire two quick shots. Or, if you see some friendly grub, feel free to start supper."

"You would like that, wouldn't you?"

Under her frown he knew she was smiling.

She studied the pistol with the odd-shaped grip. "Do you

always carry a second pistol?"

"In the summer, it's in my bag. In the winter, it's under my coat. It's always best to be prepared. Now, I'll be back as soon as I can."

The girl, not happy being left alone, flashed him a convicting eye, then turned her mount and the string of other horses down into a notch between the hillocks. Looking back she saw Crowe disappearing over a rise. Dismounting, she pulled the saddle off her horse and did the same with the others. There was little grass where she stood, so she gathered up the reins and led them over a notch in the knolls and saw a muddy circle of brackish water. But near a copse of young trees, there was enough grass to keep them satisfied.

Dropping the reins, Iron Hand followed the string of horses to the trees. The tramping of their hooves brought the sleeping Finn O'Clery awake with a start. He thought he was still drunk, or dreaming, when he saw the girl. Forgetting his pounding head, he rose stealthily to his feet. The girl was looking down, staring at the ground so the deserter managed to conceal himself in the deep shadows of the trees. He watched her, trying to recover his senses.

Iron Hand, intent on the horses, moved down among them to the trees. She had not forgotten about the two young men who had been killed by the shooter named Baby. He was the one who had ridden in and killed Uncle Pea. And then her aunt. From her hiding place, she did not see Henry Mussel killed, but she heard the shooting. She did see Bull Head fall, and it sickened her. This young rider was the one she most wanted to see killed. He was a crazy one. So deep were her sad thoughts, she did not hear or see the dark hand take hold of her long braids and yank her head back. She did feel the knife blade poke her in the side.

"Well, ain't ye a sight for a hungry man's eyes."

Iron Hand knew instantly the owner of that ugly voice.

O'Clery had poked her with the knife just enough to get her attention. Still holding her by the hair, he whispered in her ear. "If ye ain't the prettiest lil' cactus in this here desert. Why, ye plum grew outta nowheres."

The pistol. In her sudden shock, the girl had forgotten it. Gripping it tightly, she reached behind her and pulled the trigger. The explosion startled the horses, and throwing back their heads, they danced on nerve-rattled legs. The bullet barely grazed O'Clery's left side, scarcely breaking the skin, but leaving a painful powder burn against his ribs.

Still gripping her hair, he swung Iron Hand around and slapped her hard across the face. As she fell backward, he jerked the pistol out of her hand. On the ground, a thin thread of blood trickled from her lip. Angered, O'Clery fired the pistol again, burying a slug in the ground next to Iron Hand's head. Already fidgety, the horses jolted again, then stared wide-eyed at the man.

O'Clery did his own dance, hopping around on one foot, rubbing his burning side.

"Damn you, girl."

Lying prostrate inside a tuft of saw grass, Boone Crowe heard the two shots. In another instant his own Henry roared and a pronghorn bucked and fell, a clean shot through the chest. *Trouble,* he thought. Double trouble. Here lay their food. He could mark the spot and come back for it, but likely the coyotes or wolves would have it devoured before he got back. But if the girl was in danger, he had to get back to her. Even as he was considering all this, he found himself in the saddle and riding back to where he'd left her. There would be other antelope but no other Isabel.

Crowe came in on a gallop. As he rode, he prepared his mind for every possibility, and did what he could to equip himself, He saw the tips of the green trees and headed straight for them, his eyes scanning left and right. The horses were there, standing in odd tension, and then he saw two people, knowing one of them was the girl. He guessed bitterly at who the other one was. When he was closer, Crowe reined in and dismounted, keeping the Ghost Horse between himself and O'Clery.

By now the deserter was putting things together. "Are ye with him?" O'Clery demanded, but Iron Hand made no reply. He still held her by the long braid, keeping the knife blade close at hand. He had pocketed the .38 but within close reach. Gazing across the patch of brushy land that separated him from this newcomer, O'Clery considered his options. "State yer business, mister," he hollered.

Boone Crowe tried to remain calm. "The girl is my business."

O'Clery laughed. "And a jolly good thing is that, eh." He laughed again. "Well, she's with me now, old man. And she'll be a'stayin with me now." Saying this, he showed the knife and coolly placed the flat of the blade again Iron Hand's cheek. "I'd hate to ruin this lass's pretty face."

"Give it up, O'Clery."

The mention of his name startled the man. "Huh, how... who...what gives you..." He shifted uncomfortably. "Who are ye? Whaddya want with me?"

"I want the girl. Turn her loose, and you can go yer own way." He was standing in the open now, realizing the very real danger Iron Hand was in. He blamed himself for having left her alone in the first place. Seeing her now, like this, put a hot stone in his gut.

"'Pears we both want the same thing." O'Clery patted the girl's face with the flat of the blade, almost affectionately.

Boone Crowe, with each passing moment, edged closer.

"Now, tis my thinkin you'd be tossin that gun o' yers into the dirt. Right easy."

The old marshal didn't move.

O'Clery raised the knife to Iron Hand's throat now, and he made an imaginary stroke with the flat end of the blade. "I'd hate to kill this pretty lass, afore I got a chance to use her."

This news was both good and bad. At least he hadn't violated her yet. But his intent was clear. With fingertips, Crowe lifted the pistol from its holster and tossed it on the ground. In spite of the danger, looking into the girl's eyes, he could see a resolute composure there, something beyond hatred. It was the Indian in her, a courage that a proud, defeated Cheyenne people could not relinquish. She met his eyes, and in those dark pupils there was no mistaking the message. *Kill him.*

O'Clery let go of the girl's hair but kept the knife on her. Then, from his pocket, he retrieved the .38 pistol with his left hand and waved it in the air. "See here. I am a killer."

"You are a sonofabitch," Crowe returned.

O'Clery laughed. "Likely I be that also."

In his mind, Boone Crowe was measuring distance. He was measuring risk and odds and even steady handedness. But seeing the girl, unafraid now, he also saw love. What if Little Feet had not been taken from him? Could they have produced between them a daughter such as Isabel? The knot in his stomach had now moved to his throat. The pistol that lay in the dirt was not his old war Colt. He had stuffed his own familiar pistol in the back of his waistband. He had put the recovered pistol of the deceased L.P. Quinn in his holster.

By now only thirty paces separated them. With the unspoken words of motion, Crowe looked hard into the girl's eyes and tilted his body to the left, notching his head ever so slightly in the same direction. An almost indiscernible nod followed from the girl. For a moment, staring at Iron Hand, he was filled with sadness. Who would ever know the softness he held inside for her? All of his marshalling, and all the killing that had plagued him his whole life, from the war forward, yet he remained a man capable of deep compassion. For once it was not the memory of Little Feet he was seeing, rather this brave, yet troubled young woman. Could love and hate exist in the same split second? He would soon know.

O'Clery had been talking through this whole time. "...I am the butcher of Five Points. Why me brothers and me, we ruled the—"

From the back of his waistband, Crowe took a firm grip on his Colt, whipped it out, and in the fraction of a second, fired. His bullet missed Iron Hand's leaning head by four inches, striking O'Clery above the right eyebrow, taking a patch of his skull out the back. Instantly the girl sprang away, splattered with O'Clery's blood. But as the already dead O'Clery faltered on his feet, the .38 exploded, sending a stray bullet through the sleeve of Crowe's shirt. The deserter, after a spasmodic jerk, fell like a plank to the ground.

When Iron Hand had sprang away from O'Clery, she had fallen, and Crowe was immediately at her side. He saw the blood. "You hit?"

She looked up at him, shaking her head. "I don't think so. Is... is he dead?"

Crowe helped her to her feet but kept hold of her arm. "There's blood on your face."

The girl wiped at it with her hand, smearing it further. She then looked at O'Clery's twisted body, staring for a long time. "You had another gun."

He was still looking at her. Untying his kerchief from around his neck, he began wiping at the blood on her face. Iron Hand lowered her eyes. She didn't know how to react to such care.

"I shoulda never left you."

She put her hand on his arm so he would stop. "I'll wash it off," her voice wavering. "You... you..." And then she was sobbing. Boone Crowe pulled her close and let her cry. Against his chest, he felt the beating of her heart.

"Your father?"

"No. My father's friend. Well, actually...he is my friend too. Sort of. William Grandforth was one of my professors at the University of Maryland."

Paige Lacrosse was not frowning but neither was she smiling. "Apparently one of your favorites. You've talked about him."

"I have?" Rud said, surprised.

Paige finally smiled. "And now he has offered you a job."

They were sitting on the porch, and Rud Lacrosse was wearing out his hat, turning it around and around by the brim as if it were a cartwheel. "A teacher's assistant position." His voice carried a perplexed wonder to it.

"Science?"

Rud nodded. "But...but I have a job."

Paige threw her head back this time, laughing. "Rud, honey. You are the marshal of a wild country. You scarce get credit for keeping the peace."

He held up his hand. "Paige. I took an oath to the office."

"An oath superseded only by a better job. Or death by violence. Whichever comes first."

Rud finally turned and looked at her. "You sound as if you want me to take it."

"I want you to at least look into it. Talk to this Professor Grandforth."

Standing, Rud looked down the dusty street that trailed into Buffalo. "You're the daughter of the richest rancher in these parts, Paige. You'd give that up?"

"To be the wife of the handsomest assistant professor in Baltimore? I reckon I would. Are you not the same man that won me over with your fancy talk about the flight of birds? You and your speeches about the placement of the stars? Besides, I suspect you'd live a little longer writing formulas on a chalkboard than in another gunfight."

He turned and looked at her, his face still a bit puzzled. "What about this?"

"You know, Rud, if something happened to you, they'd have to find a new marshal."

"And who might that be?"

Paige rose from her chair and came to his side. "You men think you know so much. Women are the ones who work behind the scenes."

"What's that supposed to mean?"

"Don't worry. When you wire your professor friend in Baltimore, tell him your wife will be coming with you."

The silence was loud, the night so quiet it hurt Henry Mussel's ears. He had listened to Straw Dog's words, about the graves and who was in them. Or who he thought were in them. The air still carried a sickening odor of the charred wood of the old trading post. He was sure he could smell too the flesh of his friends, though he doubted that was possible. He wished it would rain. Something to make the earth new again.

Straw Dog was gone. He had left the day before. He had men to chase, he'd said. Men to capture and kill.

Gingerly Henry Mussel rose from his blankets and stood before the open flap of the tipi. Only outside did the silence get replaced by the rustling of leaves in the copse of trees where the graves lay. It was a chilling breeze, carrying no relief with it. He stood, facing away from it, eyeing the silhouette of the trees in the twilight. *Was the girl buried there too?* he wondered. He tried to remember everything about that day. Not the day of the killings. That was nothing but a blur. A bad dream. No, it was the day Iron Hand had given him the feather of a hawk. It has long been a Cheyenne belief that a hawk's feather provides protection from his enemies.

The feather was still in his tipi. Still in his medicine bag of cherished keepsakes. Had the girl sensed coming danger? Was it this hawk's feather that saved his life? Along with his brothers, the coyote pups? It was not uncommon for a young Cheyenne girl to show interest in a young man. But this girl was not like the other girls he'd known, now either dead or on reservations. Iron Hand had been at the white man's Indian school. Far away. She was only partly Cheyenne now. She had learned the white man's words. His letters. She could read. Even her speech no longer sounded like the hard prairie talk of other girls.

He had been here, working for Mr. Peacock. Breaking his mustangs. Bull Head and himself. He was here when the girl arrived from her school. A full year ago. After a while she would come to the corrals and watch the horses.

At the side of the graves he knelt now. He placed the open palm of his hand on each. Henry Mussel closed his eyes and prayed for something that would tell him if Iron Hand was among those buried there.

Chapter 12

Baby Sullivan came out of his stupor like a man drowned. He sputtered for breath, his very eyes in protest, blinking open rapidly before coming to full focus. He felt he was floating, then realized he was on a very soft bed. His waking came in fits and starts, his arms felt filled with lead. It was then that he realized he was naked and that his nakedness was lying next to more nakedness. He turned his head slowly until the globular form of Darling Annie's jiggling body came into view.

He studied her, the way someone might study a strange sea creature. She had no specific shape, other than that of kneaded bread dough. Her breasts were not huge like the rest of her, and by themselves, not unappealing. Her face, as she snored softly, looked different in this light, not so rough. Sometime, between when he took that drink of potion, Darling Annie must have bathed, for the strong odor of sweat was gone, replaced by a powdered fragrance he could only associate with some kind of flower.

His own loins ached, as if he'd ridden a bad horse over a hard trail. He only had to guess at the cause of that. Lifting his head slightly, he gave the room a quick searching, hoping to see his clothes, but he saw nothing. Slowly, he turned onto his side, hoping to sneak out of bed and flee, but instantly Darling Annie's heavy arm was thrust across his chest.

"Where you think you're going, baby honey?"

"I...jist..."

"I ain't had the likes of a young rabbit like you in a coon's age. What's yer hurry?"

Baby Sullivan stared at the ceiling. The painful act of putting thoughts together began troubling his mind. He was used to being told what to do. He remembered his own moaning just yesterday. About being lonesome. And hungry. Darling Annie wasn't the sweetheart he hoped he might find. But she was sure a sight better than talking to the prairie dogs and sage hens. So long as she kept him in grub, what was the harm? That stew she fed him was plumb better than anything the army ever give heed to. Once fattened up for a week or so, he'd light out. Maybe even with a plan.

This was the hardest thinking Baby Sullivan had ever done, and it seemed as strange to him as if he found himself suddenly sprouting wings.

"I ain't goin nowhere, Annie. Jist workin the saddle sores outta me legs."

"You just leave that to me, baby honey."

Keeping the morning sun to his right, Cletus Burke meandered northward, showing no inclination to hurry, thus saving wear and tear on his horse. Only occasionally did his thoughts wander back to the others, and when they did, it was usually about the deeds they had done. He regretted none of them. If there was one to hold to, it was for not being able to keep the Crow woman to himself. Injuns was Injuns and he had no love for them. But a woman was a woman too, and she might have made mighty welcome company till he got to Montana. After that, she would be easy to dispose of.

All these thoughts kept his mind occupied as he plodded along.

Near noon, when the sun bore down on him, he came across a trail lined with multiple wagon wheel marks in the dust, heading due west. He studied them, then let his eye follow the tracks. He removed his hat and scratched his head. *They're headin somewhere,* he thought. One wagon made sense, but not a whole passel of them. He considered all possible explanations, settling on none. But there had to be a destination, and that likely meant a town. Still, Cletus Burke was a cautious man. At some point, when Tunneson didn't return to the fort, that worthless Captain Gillespie would send a party out looking. And then there was the telegraph. It was possible that the army would put a bounty on them, attracting every bounty hunter in the territory.

Then again, he thought, *the army's probably happy to be rid of us.* And there was no love lost between Tunneson and Gillespie anyway. But looking again at the trail in the dust, he reckoned it was worth weighing the odds. He was out of whisky and near out of food. If a town was at the end of these wheel tracks, opportunity might be there too. He had a couple of dollars, enough for a meal, but no bed. He wished now that he'd followed Quinn and O'Clery and killed them both. The money they had would have tidied him over for a while. And killing them would have been a pleasure on top of it.

Burke put his hat back on his head and scratched at his whiskers. The image of a well-cooked steak and a pile of onions or potatoes toyed with his mind. And the winking amber gleam of a whisky bottle. The deal was made. He turned his horse west, come what may.

There was a knock on Judge Schaffer's chamber door. The judge raised his eyes from scanning the notes on a case soon to be placed on his docket. He stared at the door, hoping whoever knocked would go away, but a second series of knocks told him he would have no such luck. "Come in," he bellowed. Then he looked back down at his papers.

Marshal Rud Lacrosse opened the door and stepped inside. "Pardon me, Judge," he said.

Hearing Lacrosse's familiar voice, Judge Schaffer looked up, and then motioned him forward. "I'm busy. What is it?"

Rud had already removed the badge from his shirt and held it in his hand. When Schaffer still hadn't looked up, he placed it on the desk and pushed it forward.

When the judge's eyes locked on the badge, his gaze lifted, and he stared under knitted eyebrows at the young lawman.

"What's this?"

Lacrosse shifted on his feet. He'd sooner meet a man in the street for a shootout than have to suffer what he knew was coming next. "My resignation, sir."

Judge Schaffer was up and out of his chair. "Your what?"

"My resignation, sir. I'm quitting marshaling."

"Is this a joke?"

"May I sit down?"

"No. Dammit, no."

"But..."

"You can't quit. You can't *quit.*"

Rud let out a deep breath. "I just did, your honor."

"Don't 'your honor' me. I can't be without a marshal."

"You have Clayton."

"Clayton's Buffalo's sheriff. I need him there."

"Promote him to marshal."

"Are you crazy?"

"What about my deputy, Wales? He's steady."

"He's married. Damn. You're all married. And that's the trouble. Crowe quits the minute he gets married. Now you. And Wales...he's about as love sick as...oh, hell, never mind. You can't quit."

Rud crossed his arms but didn't speak.

"Did you ever find out where Boone Crowe disappeared to?"

"I told you. I think he's on a horse roundup with the army."

Schaffer moved away but then turned back. "It's the women that's ruining me."

"Sir."

"Be quiet. I need to think."

"Sir, if you'd let me explain."

The judge finally plopped back down in his chair.

"I've been offered a teaching position at my old university."

"I have a territory to run."

"Actually, sir, that's the governor's job."

"That imbecile."

Lacrosse turned to go.

"Wait. Wait. Sit down."

"I really need to go."

"Can't you wait till Crowe gets back?"

"What's Boone got to do with this?"

Schaffer tapped his fingers on the desktop. He rubbed his smoothly shaven cheeks. He'd been wearing his reading glasses and he removed them. Finally he let out a heavy sigh. "Teaching, you say. What kind of teaching?"

Rud let his own shoulders relax. "Science, sir. It's only an assistant position, but it could lead to a full professorship. Over time."

"Just like that?"

"It came as a surprise for me too. I'd be a fool not to take it. And, of course, I've already decided that I will. Me and Paige."

"Yes. Those women again."

"Is there anything else, Judge?"

"When are you leaving?"

"Within the week."

"Crowe will be disappointed to learn you've gone without seeing him. You two have been through a lot together."

"It is one of the hard parts about leaving. And Rose of Sharon is gone too. To Illinois."

The judge stood again. "You've put a load on me, son. But then, well, there's some days when I wish I could pick up again. I'm from Ohio, you know."

"No, sir, I didn't know that."

It was a moment of severe awkwardness, but finally the judge put out his hand. Surprised, Rud took a step toward the desk and took the judge's hand. "You'll be hard to replace, Lacrosse. You were a good peace officer."

"Thank you, sir."

After Rud left the chambers, shutting the door behind him, the judge pounded his fist on his desk.

When Private Bright Cohen returned to Fort Laramie with what remained of Sergeant Tunneson's original patrol, he had reported immediately to Captain Gillespie, urging him to send out a fresh patrol to assist the sergeant. It had been three or four days now since he'd watched the captain brush his request aside with the wave of a hand. *Tunneson got himself in this pickle, and he can get himself out.* It was no pickle, Cohen knew, something far worse. Sergeant Tunneson was still gone.

Every day since then, the captain had kept Cohen busy on daily short range patrols, looking for imaginary hostiles. The biggest danger from Indians in these parts was long over, and both he and the captain knew it. If only Colonel Beach would return. Tunneson was the colonel's right-hand man. And that, Private Cohen believed, was the crux of the problem.

Cohen, with a group of three other men, were riding several miles southwest of the fort, and a thought struck him. *What if I sent word back to Gillespie that we'd struck an Indian trail and we decided to follow it?* He could send the other three back and give the captain the word. Or there was Cochran. He had been a favorite of Sergeant Tunneson's. He and Cochran could feint chasing Indians, and send the other two back. And then, after another day, Cochran could go back to the fort and report Cohen killed.

Cochran would likely go along with that, he thought.

He called for a rest, and the patrol bunched together and dismounted.

"Water break," Cohen said. After a bit he and Cochran strolled into the sagebrush. "You know," he said, "these patrols are nothing more than punishment for siding with Sergeant Tunneson.

Martin Cochran spat on the ground. "Tunneson could be dead by now."

"That ain't no reason to not find him."

"True enough. I'm jist sayin, that whatever happens, it's on Gillespie's head."

Cohen shared his idea and Cochran listened. "Why don't we both jist light out?"

"Can't. They'd get us for desertin, just like those other bastards. No, one of us would have to be dead. And that'd be me. Gillespie would be happy to have me out of the way. He'd likely do nothin about it."

Cochran rubbed his chin. "What about them?" he said, tilting his head in the direction of the other two soldiers.

"They'll be glad to jist git back to the fort. We'll jist tell 'em we're going to follow a trail we seen yonder."

"What'll you do then?" Cochran said. "That's mighty big country out there."

"I'll head to Peacock's first. Unless I find a trail." He put a hand on Cochran's shoulder. "And you, you'll have to dream up a blood-curdlin story to tell Gillespie. Tell him I got scalped. Or burned at the stake. Make it good. And you got away by the skin a yer teeth."

Cochran looked at his friend. "It's plumb stupid. The whole thing. The only thing goin for it is, you're right. Gillespie'll just laugh and call it a day. He'll make a note of it in his daily report, and good-bye Private Cohen." Cochran laughed. But then he turned. "Wait. What if you find the Sarge and you bring him back? You wouldn't be dead anymore."

"Easy. Just say you thought I was dead, but I wasn't. That is, if I wanna come back. Maybe me and the sergeant will just head Calyfornia way."

It was Private Cohen's turn to laugh.

Iron Hand and Boone Crowe made camp near where he'd shot the pronghorn. Surprisingly it had been unmolested. While Boone set about butchering the animal, the girl cleared a spot for a fire. He had explained how he had replaced Quinn's pistol for his own. He didn't want to trust it to shoot straight. So that was the one he'd thrown in the dirt. His faithful war Colt was hidden behind him, and he at least knew that it shot true.

Boone had poured canteen water onto his neckerchief, and she'd scrubbed her face clean. It was back around his neck now, feeling cool on his skin. She looked at him, then moving closer gave him an awkward hug. There was a time when he might not have understood this gesture, but Rose of Sharon had taught him many things. About needs. About the value of the human touch. *Holding someone close who's been hurt, well, it's like medicine to them, Boone,* she had told him. It couldn't have been easy for this angry, damaged child to offer up such raw emotion. But he was grateful for it. It was clear that he needed it too.

Crowe skewered a hunk of roast on a green willow branch and let the fat drip and sizzle in the fire. When it was cooked through, he used his knife to cut thick slices, and they ate until it was gone.

"I was afraid."

He nodded. "It's good you can say it. Fear can be a friend sometimes." He paused. "I was afraid too. For you."

It seemed strange to celebrate a killing, but it was plain enough to both of them that killing any of these desperate men, especially Quinn and O'Clery, spared any future victims who might fall prey to them had they lived. Crowe rarely chambered more than five rounds in his Colt as a safety measure, keeping his hammer on an empty chamber while he rode. Of those five bullets, he'd used three. He had two left. Even as he reloaded his pistol now, he knew that those two were reserved for Sullivan and Burke, wherever in this wide open territory they might be now. He knew that finding them would not be easy.

While they ate, Boone had been watching the sky, noticing an increasing cluster of black clouds moving with predictable speed across the vast Wyoming landscape. Under different circumstances, he might have welcomed the prospect of rain, but this storm, once it arrived, would likely wipe out any trail they hoped to find. He knew the country, having traveled nearly every corner of it. What he wanted now was some shelter, and if memory served correctly, they would find a broad circle of plains cottonwoods several miles to the northwest.

They cleared camp and set out, leading their string of collected horses. They had left Quinn sitting upright in death, and likewise O'Clery was left where he lay, a twisted, bloody heap. Boone supposed that if the bodies were stumbled upon, there might be questions. But it was likely the wolves would get to them first.

Chapter 13

CASPER WAS A STRETCHED-OUT town with one wide street, and by the time Cletus Burke rode in under a downpour of rain, the place was wallowing in mud. The first thing he saw was a tall church steeple, but directly across the street was a livery, and he hurried his drenched horse directly to it. He reined up inside the open door and shivered, water streaming off the brim of his hat. A young boy came running from the stalls and looked him over.

"Help ya?" the boy asked.

Burke dismounted and handed the boy the reins. "He'll need a rub down. And oats. How much?"

"Ain't that much, mister. My pa will take yer money soons he gits back."

"When's that?"

"Pa's down yonder helpin set up the circus."

"Circus," grunted Burke. He walked back to the open door and peered through the gray rain to the far end of the long street. Sure enough, there was the makings of broad, colorful tents being erected out on an open field. "Well, I'll be if it ain't so."

"Yer mighty soaked, mister. And the hotel'll be fillin up fast. What with the circus and all." The boy had already removed the saddle and was standing there with a horse brush.

"What's yer name, boy?"

"Lawrence is the long of it, mister. But folks call me Low fer short."

"Low it is then. You got law in this town?"

The boy looked at him curiously. "Sure we got law."

"And a telegraph office?"

"That too," Low answered slowly. "Beggin yer pardon, mister. Are you on the run or somethin? I mean, you wouldn't be the first."

Burke waited before he answered. He wondered about the others. About O'Clery and Quinn. And that little devil, Baby Sullivan. Had any of them come this far? "No," he said with a half-smile. "I'm the one hunting."

Low felt a quiver of pleasure. "You a bounty hunter, mister?"

Here Burke's smile broadened. "Yer a clever one, lad. You got me pegged quick enough."

The boy puffed out his chest.

"And you're right about me bein soaked. Where's that hotel you spoke of?"

"Take yer pick, mister. We got three. Casper House is the biggest, and the Clairton is cheaper. And smaller." The boy pointed through the open door. "You can see the sign from here."

Burke was short on funds, so it would be the Clairton. For now. He turned and eyed the boy, who was leading the horse to a stall. "Yer pa gitten paid to help out down there?"

"Shore he is."

Cletus Burke kept that thought in his mind later, when he sat in the hotel's tub of soapy, lukewarm water. He had no other set of clothes, so he'd have to lay them out until they dried since the luxury of buying new ones would have to wait as well. But he had a plan. He would lose the beard he had while in the army, even if he had to do the job himself with his own razor. With a telegraph office here, the word may have reached Casper authorities to be on the lookout for the deserters. But then, maybe not. Hunting down army deserters was generally army business, something civil authorities showed little interest in. Unless, of course, there was a bounty on them.

While he waited for his clothes to dry, Burke stretched out on his lumpy bed and wondered about this circus. He'd seen a few back east, and he knew that they were an interesting if not utterly odd lot. On his way to the Clairton he'd seen some boys pasting up flyers on store fronts, the rain no bother to them—*The Peake & Patterson Traveling Circus of Curiosities.*

Cletus Burke's mind swam with possibilities.

The stench of the dead horses in the corral finally grew so strong that Henry Mussel set out gathering dry grass so as to start a fire substantial enough to burn the carcasses. He did this gingerly, as the wound in his side remained tender, and the last thing he wanted was to have a setback. But his tipi was here, and so, here he decided he would stay. It had been difficult work, trying to hold his breath at intervals as he made ready his pyre. He worked all day, between rests, performing this task, and by twilight he found he had nearly covered the six army horses with loose, burnable straw and saw grass.

Once lit, he moved away and watched the conflagration throw crimson flames high into the air. The carcasses themselves became flame worthy, and soon a putrid smoke rose up, throwing sparks into the darkening night sky.

Henry Mussel had no horse of his own. The mustangs had all been stolen from the corral by the men who had shot him. They would be too far away now to hunt. He wondered if Straw Dog even had much of a chance to catch the men he sought. Far to the north Henry had seen the storm gathering, but as he labored, he had watched it blow away in the distance, dropping rain everywhere but where he worked. Such was this territory. Storms were like life, he knew, bringing whatever fortune or trouble to some while leaving others untouched. Even as the sky turned dark, he could still see the heavy black pillows moving close to the earth and the slanting hard black rain beneath.

For long hours he watched the fire, his mind traveling over many thoughts.

Boone Crowe remembered the place. It was a small cluster of cottonwoods near a larger encirclement of pines and fir where he had stumbled upon the camp of bank robber, Ned Brookings and his gang, and, without questioning, had shot the outlaw and one of his partners as they sat around their campfire. But it had been a bounty hunter, Gaylord Wolfson, he was rightfully after. Wolfson had captured the wrong man, and Boone had hoped to catch up to him before something bad happened to his prisoner. Boone remembered now, bitterly, that he'd been too late to save an innocent man from being killed. But he also remembered the black wolf that seemed to have traveled with him. *Indian lore,* he thought now.

He and the girl led the string of horses deep into the copse of trees just as the first loud claps of thunder broke the still evening air. Then came flashes of lightning. And within minutes the loud pounding rain could be heard in the treetops above them, but little rain penetrated the tall trees. They picketed the horses and set up a camp in wordless concentration, each dwelling quietly on the doings of the past days. Death had ridden with them, but then, that had been the purpose of this undertaking—revenge wrapped in the tight casing of a lead and copper bullet.

Over a low fire they roasted more of the pronghorn meat, and still neither spoke. It wasn't until the coffee began bubbling over the top of the kettle that Crowe spoke. "Tell me what you know about Sergeant Tunneson."

Iron Hand, busying herself with the fire, thought for a moment. "His eyes. I remember his eyes. They were soft. Like a deer's eyes. I saw no hate in his eyes."

Crowe nodded, knowingly.

"He would look tired on his horse. Like a man...like a man who wanted shade and whisky. But he did not drink whisky. Only water. But..." She paused for a moment, and in that moment a smile curled lightly at her mouth. "But when he saw the Turtle Woman, he..." she suddenly laughed sweetly, "...he looked like a little boy. No longer tired."

The girl's words were painful to hear, but they were words he needed to hear. Regardless of his bad death, Lancelot had moments of earlier happiness. Crowe's hope now was that his friend had been dead before the woman he loved was raped and murdered. He knew there was no fear of him losing his hatred of the men he was tracking. Torture would be too kind of a judgement for them. And yet, no such pleasure had come to them. He had shot Pup Murphy so quickly, and in such a fit of rage, that there had been little thought at all put into it. The other two had also died too quickly.

Boone Crowe stood suddenly. These were bad thoughts. Bad imaginings. The face of Rose of Sharon came into his mind, and even here, near the same place he had shot and killed other outlaws, he felt ashamed of his own bitterness. But in his holster was his ugly war Colt, and it seemed to have its own voice tonight, between the claps of thunder and the pounding rain—two bullets left.

He heard the girl come up and stand beside him. She did not speak but only stood there, and he wondered if her own thoughts were likely similar to his own. Peacock, whether her true uncle or not, had been the one white man who had shown her love. Finally she touched Crowe's sleeve. "The meat is done."

They ate, sitting across from each other, the fire between them, and Boone saw how the fire cast light on her face. Surely there was a fair share of old, worn-out squaws among the Cheyenne race, but he knew full well that there were more who possessed great natural beauty. Little Feet had been one of them. And Iron Hand was one of them also. He studied her white man's brown trousers and decorated leather poncho. She had an elk robe that she had escaped the fire with, and she used it to wrap around her shoulders on cold nights. But the girl's moccasins were pure Indian, the soles already tanned black from months, maybe even years, of walking use.

"Tell me about your wife," the girl asked.

Boone offered a slow, thoughtful nod. "She's better than I deserve."

"I knew you would talk like that. Uncle Pea used to say the same thing."

"Plain truth. Likely for yer uncle too. We're wild men, tamed by women. You'll git yer chance, sooner or later."

113

He studied her face but the fire, which threw shadows, made it hard to read. Finally she said, "Once. Maybe."

Boone Crowe was not good at speeches, but he felt the girl deserved one. "I told you about Little Feet. And how I lost her. There was another woman. Eva. I lost her too. So, Rose came when...well, I guess all hope was lost. Romance does not often come to old men. But you are young. It'll come."

"Is Rose young?"

"Younger than me by a long stretch."

"And pretty, I bet."

"Prettier than a Wyoming sunset." Crowe felt suddenly foolish, tossing out words like he was some kind of poet.

Iron Hand laughed. "You sure sound like someone in love." She drew quiet herself then, thinking backward in time. After several long minutes, she spoke again. "Girls have dreams too. Dreams that don't come true. I have had them."

The rain continued through occasional, distancing thunder, and Boone Crowe thought this was a suitable place for melancholy thinking. If he could trade this rain for hot, burning smoke, it might be the Wilderness, where he and his cavalry were set on an impossible struggle all those years back. This surely was a place for ghosts; even if a man didn't believe in them, there were still ghosts aplenty lurking about. Looking at the girl, he wondered if one of Peacock's young horse breakers had been one of those lost dreams she spoke of. He remembered his friend, Axel Harrington. How he had fallen in love with the pretty little Piute girl. It happened, but not often. Not for an Indian girl.

"My friend, the one-armed preacher, he says, 'God is a God of surprises'." He looked at the girl. "I reckon that's what we got to hold on to."

The girl made no answer.

In the middle of the night, Boone Crowe woke to silence. The rain had quit its wild threshing in the treetops, and even the wind had lay down. Iron Hand was a mere, quiet shape in the darkness. He wondered—if he could ever count that high—how many times he had slept on the hard ground like this, chasing after men who deserved chasing—the bad men, when the chasing was long, like this chase was likely to be. The girl had lost a lot, but was it enough to keep her chasing with him? What if it took them into winter? Rose of Sharon would be back from Illinois long before that. He'd simply have to leave word with her that this was something he had to do.

He tried to think like an outlaw. Like a deserter on the run. What made the most sense was to get as far away as fast as he could. But there were problems with that, and money was usually the chief one. Iron Hand had dug up Peacock's hidden money box, which likely meant that Cletus Burke and the other cutthroats didn't reap much in their thievery and killing. He could only imagine the drunken passion that went into it, absent of any thought-out planning. It started with the killing of Lancelot, and the lust for blood just grew out of it.

North, he thought. Somewhere that might promise money. Or opportunity to get money, legally or illegally. That's where a half-ass thinking man might go. If Burke was the planner of the whole desertion thing, then he was probably the one most likely to head north. Montana, where all the silver, copper, and gold talk was going on. But Boone remembered something that L. P. Quinn had said in his dying moments—*Burke took off alone. Wantin no part o' the rest o' us.* That meant two trackings. It meant that Baby Sullivan was alone.

Boone settled on the notion that Burke would head north. But Sullivan, maybe not. Iron Hand said that Baby Sullivan was the one who did most of the killing. He'd ridden in and killed Bull Head, Henry Mussel, and Peacock and his wife in a burst of gunfire that happened so fast, it had taken long, hard minutes to reason it all out. And from her hiding place in the sealed closet, she had determined that Baby Sullivan was the most dangerous because he was the stupidest.

Boone had thought like Cletus Burke, now he had to think like Baby Sullivan, and the only thing that came to mind was...

direction. The kid needed direction. He needed someone to tell him what to do because that's all he'd been used to in the army.

Listening, he heard the faint clicking of a cricket in the deep, cool foliage. He closed his eyes. Baby Sullivan would be close. He would be close because he had no one to tell him what better to do. After all, he wasn't called Baby for no other reason.

Darling Annie waddled her excessive bulk out onto the boardwalk where Baby Sullivan sat, puffing on a cigar and admiring the muddy street. The little town had caught a corner of the passing storm, just enough to turn the roads into a mucky paste. The two old timers he had met the day before when he rode into town sat across the street, exchanging clever remarks at the expense of Darling Annie's latest victim.

"Here, Baby," she said, handing him a bowl of steaming chili, beans big as almonds.

Annie had fallen back into her old sweaty self again, and Baby hoped it was only because she'd been working in the hot kitchen. Her voice was still sweet as a lark bird, but in the light of day, a certain kind of terror had returned. He wondered if she had any kind of money and what kind of promises it would take to get his hands on some of it. *Not yet,* he thought. He'd been hard pressed to formulate a plan yet, and until he did, this was as good a place as any. Surely Darling Annie would not be damaged by taking another bath tonight before resuming their sleeping arrangements.

There was no bank here and few businesses that weren't closed up half the time. It was surely an end of the trail town, a place for picking your teeth and spitting tobacco juice. *And dying,* he thought. Baby couldn't even remember the name of the place, if he'd ever even heard it spoke. Maybe it had no name. He decided in his mind that a name didn't matter. A name would tie him to something, and this was not a *something* he wanted to be tied to.

His remembrances of New York City and Five Points turned vague. He had been young then, but he felt young still. He made a guess once and decided he was nearing twenty and still not a whisker to be found on his baby face. What did remain vivid was his killing of the first Indians he'd ever seen, that buck coming out of his tipi. And then the other. *Finally old Peacock hisself,* he thought. *And the woman.* That was blood he remembered and would always remember. If he ever found his way back to New York, he could puff out his chest and tell the whole damn story.

"What's ya thinkin, Baby?" It was Darling Annie's birdsong voice.

"Glory," he said. "Meself is thinkin on glory."

Chapter 14

THE RAIN HAD TURNED every low depression on the land into a wide, shallow stream. Even the horses welcomed the sunshine, and they dipped their noses in every little brook they came upon. The ground was soft and the going slow, but Crowe had a feel for the country and was gathering a feel for their mission as well. Of this he had shared nary a word. He didn't want to say it and then be wrong in the end. The girl appeared to trust him, and he didn't want that to change.

Wyoming Territory was marked by a dozen cow towns, some big, like Cheyenne, others smaller, but none worth a notice except when the cowpunchers came to town for whisky and card games. Some had whores, and some didn't, but on the scratch surface of it, they were all the same—sleepy one day and a noisy howling of hell the next. It was nothing like Dodge or Abilene, as stories went, but the need was the same—get rid of the slim money they'd just earned on all matter off useless things.

They rode with the sun to their backs for several more hours, and then, as if to prove his point, over a grassy rise they spied a branding party on the flat meadow below. They reined in and took stock. There was a rail corral, the thin gray tail of a branding fire's smoke, and a circle of six or seven punchers busy wrangling calves and putting the hot poker to the bawling beast's hide. The cowboy's horses were unsaddled and left to graze nearby, and off a ways was a cook's chuck wagon.

Iron Hand caught Boone Crowe grinning. "Something funny?"

"Might be. Let's go have a look."

They came off the little hill and headed straight for the chuck wagon. As they rode in a couple of the punchers lifted their heads and dipped their hats in his direction. The girl too made for curious viewing. Crowe had seen a heap of chuck wagon cooks in his days, but he knew this one at sight. It was the most recognizable trap of cookery on the Wyoming plains. Another thread of smoke rose from the backend of the wagon, and as they stirred their horses around, they saw a man bent over four hanging black kettles swinging from a fashioned crossbar. The lid was off a Dutch oven, revealing a circle of golden biscuits, and in the other kettles, spoons stood out on the rims like ships masts.

"Not yet," the cook called over his shoulder, without looking, his voice raspy as a rusty gate. "I'll ring the bell when it's done."

Boone Crowe continued smiling. And waiting. The cook was wrapped in a greasy apron, and his broke-down hat sat cockeyed on his graying head. He gave a final stir to every dangling pot, then finally, with hands on hips, he turned. Leaning back he looked into the old marshal's face.

"Well, I'll be a blue hen on Sunday. Boone Crowe, you devil in chaps." He moved in close to the Ghost Horse, and the two men shook vigorously. Then his eyes turned to the girl.

"Isabel," Crowe said, "this is Buckboard Bob Ottmar, the chief poisoner of the prairie."

Buckboard Bob removed his hat and bowed.

Iron Hand felt a sudden alien thrill pass through her. Her old escort had called her Isabel again, putting a strange fondness to the sound of it. But never, in her entire life, had a stranger, much less a white man, ever honored her with a bow. She flushed.

"I ain't poisoned a soul, Boone, you star-packin liar." He grinned this through a bushy mustache.

"Star's gone, Bob."

Bob Ottmar puzzled over this. "What's up?"

"Trackin some army deserters. They killed..." And suddenly there was a catch in his throat. He wrestled the rest out in a low tone. "Lancelot Tunneson."

Bob showed alarm. "That bluecoat friend of yers?"

Crowe nodded. "They burned out Peacock too. Killed him and his woman. Some others. We tracked and killed four so far. But I won't rest..."

Ottmar sensed the difficulty of the moment and waved his hand, as if to brush it away. "It's another ten minutes before I

120

clang the bell for these yahoos. I'll give you two the honor of sampling the wares before these stinky hoodlums stampede us."

Crowe knew that there wasn't a roundup, makeshift rodeo, branding party, or even a cowboy wedding that Buckboard Bob Ottmar had not made his presence known. He had recipes he guarded with his life, including a locked cabinet of spices he'd brought up from the far reaches, like New Orleans or Santa Fe, and which he shook, poured, or sprinkled into his steaming kettle. But Crowe also knew that Bob Ottmar would give you the shirt off his back if you needed it. Crowe had seen him do it.

Dismounting, Boone and the girl walked off their saddle stiffness as Bob piled up two tin plates with beans and hash, fried apples, and a warm biscuit. While they ate they talked, starting with the old days and ending with the business at hand. "Deserters, you say," Bob said.

The girl took her plate and wandered off to a shade tree, and so Boone gave Bob the details. "It was butchery at its worst," he said. "Worse than I've seen in a long while. And senseless. Bloodlust is what it was." He let this stick as he slowly stirred his beans.

Bob nodded. "Not since Custer." He looked at Crowe thoughtfully. "And some would say that was justified. Depending on whose side you're takin." He paused with the hash spoon lifted like a standard. "There always seems to be a message in killing like that."

As they talked Bob nodded toward the girl. A small black dog had wandered over in a curious way and sat in the grass at her feet. Its long nose lifted up and stared into Iron Hand's face.

"Yours?" Crowe asked.

Bob shook his head. "Started following me a couple of days ago. A beggar. Story came down that a puncher took a hoof to the head. Killed. Mighta been his. You know how dogs are. If only woman were that loyal, why they'd...well...anyway."

"It's best I'm not packin that star, Bob. I've been steppin outside the law this past week."

121

"Sometimes a man's gotta."

Boone remembered meeting Bob Ottmar before he was Buckboard Bob. He packed his own star once. A sheriff's star, down by Denver. Now he only arrested the hungry appetites of cowboys and bronc busters.

"This is pretty small fixins for you, ain't it?"

"I jist stumbled on these boys yesterday. They looked half-starved, the way most line riders do. I figured I'd give 'em at least one square meal before moving on."

"What's next?"

Bob removed his sweat-lined hat and wiped his forehead with a bandana. "Circus."

"Circus?"

"Saw the wagons and their getup heading toward Casper. Figured I might open up shop for a few days. Peake and Patterson, or some such nonsense. That's what was printed on the side of their wagons. Tents and the whole riggin." He said this while watching the girl. She had finished her food and was sitting down in the grass now, petting the little black dog. Boone followed his gaze.

"Girl's my eyes," Crowe said. "She saw the killers close up. I need her to identify them."

"Before you kill them?"

"You know how it is, Bob."

"I do. I do know and I attach no guilt to it. Snakes were meant to be stepped on. The Lord did that in Gethsemane. Heel to the head." Buckboard Bob spoke this with stern conviction.

"I need more than the girl's eyes, Bob. Maybe she can give you a word or two on what these last two look like. A travelin man like you just might see something."

They went to the girl and listened as she gave Bob a thin sketch of Baby Sullivan and Cletus Burke's recognizable features. Baby, she said, had hair red as a carrot with a deceivingly innocent face full of freckles. Burke, he was nearly six feet tall, a little shorter than Boone. She then tugged at her right earlobe. "It is gone," she said. "This part of his ear is gone."

Bob looked at Crowe. "Well, I'll keep my eyes open. How'll I get back to you if I see something?"

The old marshal stroked his whiskers. "Leave a message with the livery man. They usually know more than the lawmen do. Or the bankers. Or just about anybody else." He nodded toward Iron Hand. "We'll check some cow towns. Then head Casper way after that. I appreciate it, Bob."

They looked at the girl. The dog was licking her hand.

"Let's trade favors," Bob said. "I'll keep an eye peeled for your deserters. You take the dog off my hands."

"A dog is the last thing I need."

"You speaking for yourself. Or for the girl. Look at those two."

Boone Crowe took two cigars out of his vest pocket and offered one to Bob. A match was struck, and they blew smoke in short puffs into the wind. "You drive a hard bargain. Ask the girl. If she says yes, we'll take the dog. Critter got a name?"

"I've only had her less than a week. But...well, I've been calling her Margot."

"Margot? After who?"

Bob laughed. In his gravelly voice he said, "You don't need to know everything."

Buckboard Bob rang the dinner bell, and the cowboys threw down their irons and gathered around, tin plates extended.

Back in their saddles, Boone Crowe and Iron Hand headed west, the little black dog cradled like a child against the girl's belly and the horn.

Every day Rud Lacrosse watched the horizon for the return of Boone Crowe but to no avail. The prairie landscape seemed especially barren lately. *A watched pot never boils*, he took himself to thinking, but he watched anyway. He had taken care of the formalities by way of telegram, of making a formal, though somewhat tentative, acceptance of the assistant teaching position; of informing his father of his impending journey by train, with wife, Paige; and a word of thanks to his former professor for considering him. Their bags were essentially packed, or stored away, and the greater portion or their good-byes spoken. All but Boone Crowe.

He had postponed their departure already by several days, and still no Boone. It seemed an insult to leave without seeing him, but it was clear that to wait any longer would be imprudent. So at last the tickets had been purchased, and this afternoon they would leave Buffalo by stage to the railhead at Fort Tillman and ride out of the Wyoming Territory the same way he had arrived, though a much-changed man. He had ridden at Boone Crowe's side for five years, from the time the old marshal had drawn him back into lawing.

Having been nearly hanged by a violent cattleman named Starkweather, Lacrosse had pulled off his badge and melted into the shadows. It was Boone who had erased both his shame and his fear, pinning the badge back on him. Starkweather was long gone now, as were a whole trail of outlaws, gunmen, and rustlers they had tracked down and either jailed or killed. The killing was the hard part, and easily the part he was now happy to give up. But Boone Crowe deserved better than an absent good-bye. Still...

Rud Lacrosse stared down at the letter he had finally grown weary of rewriting and settled on it as the best he could do. Folding it, he slid it into a plain envelope and wrote the old marshal's name across the front. He would ride it out to Boone's little ranch and leave it in the care of old Rufus, Boone's toothless hired hand, left to watch over things in Rose of Sharon's and Boone's absence. Toothless as he was, and a permanent limp from his days as a prisoner during the State's war, he possessed a sharp mind for detail and a tremendous loyalty to Crowe.

The stage was a half hour late, but Rud and Paige made Fort Tillman just as the sun was throwing a blood red gloaming across the land. After a brief farewell to the one-armed preacher, who held court among the whores and wobegones of the rail town, they finally found themselves standing on the train platform. Rud took a long, thoughtful look into a land that had shaped him. A land both hard and beautiful. Paige's family was ranchers with a large spread and many cows to manage, so Rud knew they would come back for visits. But it would be different. Time always made things different.

The circus tents were up, the brightly striped canvases looking like something otherworldly on this otherwise wilderness of tall grass, antelope, and distant mountains. The streets, still muddy from the rain, were filled with children racing back and forth in high excitement for when the tents threw back their flaps for the official opening. A strange odor had risen from the animal cages, where an occasional growl or shriek rolled out from between the wagons, sending up an ever-heightening thrill that seeped through the expecting townsfolk.

In the middle of this strange new world strode Cletus Burke. Either by chance or by purpose, Burke had found himself at supper seated at a table directly next to the ample-bellied Amos Peake and Thurgood Patterson, the very men responsible for turning Casper into a sideshow frenzy of anticipation. Cletus Burke, if he was not good at much, was clearly a master at lying. By fraudulent tale-telling, he introduced himself as a railroad agent on the trail of a villain.

"I have reason to believe he is somewhere here, in Casper. No doubt lurking in the shadows," Burke said, straight faced. "Your circus could be a perfect cover for him. But..." He smiled with an air of preeminence. "But a perfect cover for myself as well." He let those words sink in, feeling falsely confident.

"That's quite a fable, Mister...what did you say your name was?" This from Amos Peake.

Burke felt immediately rebuffed. "I didn't give it. Fable or not.

We shall see." He stood to leave but was stopped by a hand from Thurgood Patterson.

"Sit," Patterson said. Unseen by Burke, he flashed a humorous wink at Peake. "Now. Tell us more. I'm intrigued. Who is this... this villain, as you call him? Is he dangerous?"

This was Burke's chance if he were to have one. Collecting himself, he said, "Name's Ferguson. Flanner Ferguson. Agent with the Pacific Railway. I'm trailing a man...well, boy really. His name is Sullivan. Goes by Baby Sullivan."

"And you think he might be lurking around Casper?" Peake's persistently smiling face was hard to read.

"It's where his trail has ended. Here. Yes."

"And you want what from Mr. Patterson and myself? Exactly."

Burke took a deep breath. "Truth be told, gentlemen... practically nothing. I can't afford to stay here long if it becomes evident that Baby Sullivan isn't here. He doesn't know who I am or what I look like. But I know very well what he looks like. So, all I would ask of you is to allow me the freedom of roaming among both your temporary workers and your circus goers. The paying customers. The more faces I see, the quicker I can either root him out or confess defeat and move on myself." These were the same kind of lies he had told to get him into the army. Fabricating a false past and identity, possessing just enough schooling to know how to sound convincing.

Peake and Patterson looked at each other. "What's this Baby villain look like exactly?"

"A baby-faced redhead. Barely twenty. Freckles."

Patterson looked doubtful, but he spoke in an even tone. "We'll be here three days, Mr. Ferguson. Starting tomorrow. We'll grant you one day of mingling with the crowd. One day is all. Wherever we go, we encounter pickpockets and conmen. Sometimes con-women. If you are a man of the law, well, we would appreciate it if you'd keep those busy eyes of yours on the lookout for *our* interests as well. You have one day."

And so it was, as the sun was making a comeback from the

previous day's storm, Cletus Burke strolled with an official bearing, giving off an air of secret authority. He was determined to make good of this one day's window of opportunity. He wasn't interested in getting rich, only traveling money. Enough to get him to Montana. And, if by some stroke of luck he did find Baby Sullivan slinking around, he would have the added pleasure of killing him.

As for Peake and Patterson. They knew a conman when they saw one. After all, they were the biggest conmen in the business. "He's got more on his mind than chasing some imaginary outlaw," Peake said.

Patterson agreed. "Let's put Decius on his track."

His partner nodded. "If he tries to steal anything. Anything at all, tell Decius to break his arm."

Chapter 15

PRIVATE BRIGHT COHEN HAD seen the red glow in the distance and calculated it was old Amadeus Peacock's trading post, the very place he was heading. He had sent Martin Cochran back to Fort Laramie with the fabricated story of his demise by Indians. He had no idea if the scam had worked, but it was too late now to wonder. If he didn't find the sergeant, he hoped he would at least find some answers. But this fire in the distance was a sure sign that something was up.

He rode for another hour in the dark until he finally crossed into a side wind, carrying the putrid stench of burning flesh and hair. He tried to see the trading post in the dim moonlight, but he could not see it. The fire, which was now just a smoldering of red coals, were not where the post had been, rather in the corral. He knew the place from patrols with Tunneson, but there was definitely something different about it now.

Riding into the yard he saw plainly now, even in the dark, the ash heap that had once been Peacock's store. And where there had once been two tipis for his horse breakers, there was now only one. The other, like the trading post, had been reduced to ruin. The fire, he realized, was either horse flesh or worse, human flesh. Cohen pulled his carbine from its sheath and peered deeper into the menacing circle of the yard.

Then, from the shadows, came a voice. "Name yourself."

Cohen knew that voice. He had stood with Tunneson on several occasions, boots on the bottom rung of the corral, watching Henry Mussel and Bull Head pounding or getting pounded by green unbroken horses. They did what Cohen knew he never could.

"Henry? Is that you?"

There was a long silence.

"It's me. Private Cohen. I'm looking for the sergeant."

The voice was stern and steady. "Dead."

"Who's dead?"

"All dead."

Here was the fear that Cohen had harbored. *All dead*, he repeated in his head, and it sickened him. "May I dismount?" He asked this out of courtesy.

Like a ghost, Henry Mussel appeared suddenly out of the gloom. The Indian put his hand on the neck of Cohen's horse and stroked gently. Cohen climbed down from the saddle, and the two young men sized each other up, the gleam of their eyes the only things visible.

"Murdered?" Cohen asked.

Henry nodded. "Army."

"Deserters," Cohen said. "Bad men. Very bad."

"They kill sergeant. Shoot me. Kill Bull Head. Kill Peacock and women."

"How'd you make it?"

"Shoshone."

Cohen nodded. "Straw Dog. Where is he now?"

"Leave. Help me. Then leave. Go hunt soldiers who kill."

They walked as they talked, Cohen leading his horse. He found a post and hitched the reins to it. "Where are they? Did they burn up?"

"Graves. By trees. There." He pointed.

"Who buried them?"

Henry Mussel shrugged. "Shoshone say crow man."

Bright Cohen scratched his virgin beard. *Crow man?* Then he understood. "Boone Crowe."

Henry nodded.

Private Cohen took some meager rations from his saddle bag, and the two men spent the rest of the night exchanging what details they knew, Henry telling what he saw before crawling to the coyote den, and Bright Cohen about his scheme of playing massacred. Two grievous men with one horse and no place to go.

In the middle of the night two cowpunchers drifted into town, and after drinking himself stupid, Baby Sullivan stumbled off to bed. In the early hours of morning, he heard Darling Annie in the next room servicing the two punchers. He lay awake, listening, and an odd sensation floated through his whisky-logged brain. It was a strange feeling, and he wasn't sure what to make of it. Is this what jealously felt like?

Baby swung out of bed and put his ear to the door adjoining the two rooms. Sure enough, the squeaking springs of the bed shrieked louder than a broke-down buckboard, as if pleading for mercy. And Darling Annie's sweet voice made a chorus of pleasurable sounds. Moans they were. An early sun was breaking the eastern ridgeline and was just then creeping through the curtained window. He found his pistol hanging from a hook by the closet. The wooden grip felt cool in his hand. And heavy. *But who to kill?* he wondered. *The cowboys? Or Darling Annie?*

He tried the knob, and it turned but the door did not give. Something was blocking it. He pressed more firmly, and it gave way with a clatter. Baby burst through, a red-eyed bull, and without a blink of thought, fired at the first thing he saw. One of the cowboys was just pulling up his pants, and the bullet caught him in the side, tossing blood and a cry. The other man, asleep on the floor, shot up out of his stupor and scrambled on the floor, making for the door. Baby shot and missed.

The first man, pants fallen back down to his knees, fumbled on the floor for his pistol. Baby shot him again; the bullet passed into the top of his head, splitting his skull. The other man had crawled out the door and was in hot flight down the stairs. Throughout this, Darling Annie was not silent. Arms up, waving, naked as the day she was born. She was crying for Baby to stop. But when Baby turned his pistol on her, Annie brazenly crossed the floor and knocked Baby senseless with a ham-sized fist.

It was an hour before Baby Sullivan came to. He was leaning against the wall of the room he'd slept in. Someone had dragged him there. His neck felt half-twisted off, and his left eye was

131

swollen shut. He only vaguely remembered what he'd done. The acrid smell of gunpowder was still strong in the air. He closed his eyes again, and the next thing he knew he was being yanked off the floor by a strong hand. It was Darling Annie, and she was so close their noses almost touched.

She hissed. "Tell me that was for love."

He blinked.

She thrust her massive arm against his chest, pinning him to the wall. "I know that boy. He was a regular. And I know who he works for. His boss is going to be here before the sun goes down. And you will be dead."

Baby blinked again.

The second cowpuncher, the one who'd managed his escape, was already halfway across the prairie, galloping at full tilt. Ahead he saw two riders, leading a string of horses. As he drew closer, he made out an old man and a young Indian girl. The girl held a dog in her lap. The old man raised a hand and motioned for him to stop.

"Yer horse got a bur?" Crowe hollered.

The cowboy's horse was in a lather and danced a couple of circles before settling down. The kid struggled to find his voice, finally blurting, "My pard jist got murdered."

"What's this?"

"Back yonder. At Duck Trap. We was...hell...jist getting some..." He eyed the girl and twisted his mouth in confused hesitation. "Some madman busted in and started shootin. Killed Chet. I crawled. I mean I crawled like I never crawled afore. Liked a'killed me too had I not."

"Where's this place?"

The kid shook his head, trying to get his senses. He threw a thumb over his shoulder. "Couple miles."

"Who was the shooter?"

"Hell, mister. I only saw him for a second. But...I think he mighta been the feller at the bar the night before. Drinkin alone."

"What did he look like?"

The kid shook his head. He gave a mock laugh. "Not more 'n a kid. Looked like his hair was on fire. Red as a carrot, it was."

Boone shot a look at Iron Hand. Her eyes were wide circles, black with fury.

"Was he armed?"

"Had a big Colt. Like them soldiers use." He glanced at Boone's war Colt. "Like yours. It was shoved in a holster that had a flap on it, like some cavalry holster. He—"

"And freckles." It wasn't a question.

"Like a shotgun blast."

"Was he alone?"

"He was last night."

Crowe looked at the wrangler's horse, its head down. "I doubt you want to kill your critter. Ain't nothin chasin you. Not likely. Get down and settle yer nerves. Yer hoss'll thank you."

"But my boss."

"Another hour won't change the outcome."

By the time the young cowpuncher had dismounted, Boone Crowe and Iron Hand were already making tracks for Duck Trap. Boone had been there before and knew it could hardly be called a town. A dumping ground for thirsty cowhands settling for gut-rotting whisky and poor eats. But it was tame. It didn't seem a place for gun play, least of all murder. It wasn't an outlaw hold-out, just a speck on the flat, sagebrush-covered plains. But if the scared young wrangler was right, Baby Sullivan just might be there.

Iron Hand's face was set like stone. All things around her had vanished, only the red rage of memory filled her. Uncle Pea had always worried about her. He didn't want anybody, especially the army troopers, to see her. He knew the trouble a young girl could make in the minds of women-starved men. He welcomed their trade, but his young niece was not to be part of the bargain.

133

So, at the first sight of the soldier riding into the yard, the last thing Uncle Pea had done for her, was lock her in the secret place. Only moments later, through the crack in the concealed door, she saw Amadeus Peacock gunned down. And then her aunt. After that, she saw everything. And she knew who had killed them and who had killed Bull Head and Henry. It was this mad red-headed animal called Baby.

Today she would watch him die.

Darling Annie herself had carried the killed cowpuncher from her room down to the back room of her little squat house, out the door of her odious kitchen, and after stopping to catch her breath, had dropped him in the dust. *Chet Byers,* she thought, remorsefully. *How many times?* she wondered. Of all the passers-through, he had always been her favorite. Gentle as a cottontail rabbit. His once beautiful head split now like a piece of stove wood and bloody as a kilt hog. The more she looked at him, the sadder she became. *That damn Baby.*

She stomped back into her kitchen and slumped at her table, her beefy arms resting heavy on the table. *And what to do now?* she wondered? From the other room she could hear Baby descending the creaky stairs. She listened as his boot heels scraped the floor. He had to go. Before all hell broke loose. Chet's boss, when he got there, would hang Baby. She knew that. And she knew too that even if she sent him away, they would find him. It was a hole he had dug for himself.

"Annie." Baby's voice sounded like a hammer on an anvil. It was fear and anger mixed. "Annie. Where be ya?"

She said nothing. Finally, looking up, she saw him in the doorway. He was holding his pistol. So this was how it was going to end.

"I need money."

Annie didn't move. She had lowered her head again and

stared at the table top.

"I know you got some." His free hand went up to his swollen face. "Me ain't got but one good eye. Thanks to you, bitch."

The word cut into Darling Annie. Deep. In all her years of whoring, no one had ever used that word against her. "Please don't call me that." He voice, as usual, was the voice of an innocent.

"Bitch," he said again. Then, "Money. Where'd ya hide it? Dammit. I gotta go. I need it...*now!*" He stepped to the table and pounded the butt of his pistol down with a loud thud. Then, as if moving on ropes and pulleys, he turned mechanically so his pistol pointed directly at Annie's face.

Annie started to speak but instead felt the barrel of the pistol smash against her temple. It turned her head, but she did not fall.

"That's fer what ye did to me face."

Darling Annie had not cried in years. Her life had been too hard to even waste on self-sympathy, but here they came, first slow, then hard, wet tears. They flooded her face, soundlessly. Even in her misery, her quiet sobs possessed a strange sweetness.

Baby was unmoved. He stepped up to strike her again when he heard the sound of horses in the street. It froze him. *The damn rancher,* he thought. *Come to kill me.* He moved back into the dingy parlor and looked out the window. Two riders. A man and a girl. If the man were there to kill him, why'd he bring a damn girl along? And an Indian girl? He puzzled over this, watching as they dismounted. His own horse was in the livery, or what stood for it. *I'll have to make a go of it,* he thought. He didn't believe this was the rancher, just some old fellow with an Indian gal.

Baby turned back and stared into the kitchen. Annie was no longer sitting at the table. Furious, he glanced once more out the window and saw the riders talking to the two old boardwalk gossips in their rocking chairs. One of them was pointing. Pointing directly at him.

"Bastards," he hissed.

The kitchen was empty when he got there, but the backdoor

was yawning open. He looked around the room in a panic. Money. Where would she hide her money? He started pulling open drawers, knocking over the pathetic vases of dead flowers, emptying canisters. Nothing.

Outside, Boone Crowe and Iron Hand followed the old man's extended arm. Passing the Ghost Horse, he fished the birdseye revolver from his saddlebag, the one he'd given the girl once before when they'd encountered O'Clery. He held it out to her. "No bravery. Understand? Just keep it for protection. But I need to know if it's him. Just don't get in the way." They started across the street but then he stopped. Crowe put his hand on her shoulder and forced himself to look square into her eyes. His voice was tight with emotion. "Listen to me. Please. I...I don't want you hurt."

Iron Hand stared back, meeting his gaze. She drew in a breath and nodded.

At the front door they could hear the clatter of banging pans and cans from farther inside. Boone turned the knob and with pistol drawn, stepped through the door with the girl following. The floor creaked, and the banging in the kitchen stopped.

"Who's...who's there?" Baby's voice quavered.

"Baby Sullivan," Crowe said. "Show yerself."

"Like...like hell." An arm came around the door jamb and a pistol roared, shooting flames. The slug struck the wall over Crowe's right shoulder. Then Crowe heard the boot heels of escape.

"Stay here," Boone said. When he entered the kitchen, he saw a fleeting glimpse of a pant leg and boot going out the door. But the girl didn't stay; she followed close at the old marshal's back as he burst out the back door. Into the light, the scene before them turned suddenly surreal. Some thirty feet away, facing them, was the redheaded deserter, a pistol extended in a shaky hand. Near him, in the dirt, knelt a very large woman, hair a mess of brown sweat curls, a face of tears, showing the red welt of a beating. And cradled in her arms was the body of a young buckaroo, head blown nearly half-off.

"It's him," Iron Hand whispered.

Baby Sullivan seemed in a fog, uneasy on his feet. The pistol in his hand was trembling inches from Darling Annie's head. His eyes were dull, his own destroyed face looking black in the sunlight. "She won't give me no money."

"Move away, Sullivan."

Annie showed no emotion. She too appeared in shock. Or, resolute to her own death.

Crowe felt the girl at his side tense up. He feared she might do her own shooting. He slowly moved his left arm in front of her as a feeble barrier. "Don't," he said.

The air felt thick. Even the birds, which had been carrying on a racket earlier, were silent. Waiting. The whole world it seemed was waiting. A soft breeze lifted a corner of Annie's worn-out dress, and the soft flutter of a dragonfly sputtered down the middle of the scene, as if a prop in a stage play. Suddenly, behind Sullivan, Boone Crowe saw the shadowy ghost of Lancelot Tunneson. His hat was off, and a few loose strands of hair seemed to lift from his forehead. His mustache was as it always was, walrus big and showing flecks of gray. Then slowly, as if giving one last command, Lancelot Tunneson's image turned its head, as if looking away.

Boone Crowe shot once, and the bullet knocked Baby Sullivan hard, backward into the dirt. The sound of the report seemed to take forever to arrive, but when it did, it felt as if the whole town might collapse under its weight. The young, murderous deserter, lay flat out now, arms stretched, as if hoping to fly away. He had been too busy watching the dragonfly to know he was a breadth away from dying.

Iron Hand moved around Boone and stood over Sullivan. Turning, she gave the birdseye pistol back to Crowe, then motioned for him to give her his hunting knife, the one fastened to his belt. He knew what she wanted and why. He hesitated, but finally, after a reluctant moment, he removed it from its sheath and handed it to her.

Boone Crowe turned away, but he could still hear the knife cutting through the crown of Baby Sullivan's head, and the sickening sound of the red-haired scalp being ripped away. He hoped it was her last savage act. He hoped that it would appease the ghosts of her past, of Willow Creek, of the white man's Indian school, of all the deaths at Peacock's trading post. It was savage, but it told a thousand stories of revenge and hatred that had passed between two kinds of different people. Different, and yet the same.

The gunshot had brought a handful of citizens bowling around the corner. They stopped, mouths gaping, trying to make out the meaning of things. A few furious eyes directed at Iron Hand were quickly quelled by the waving of Boone Crowe's old ugly war Colt.

"Help that lady to her feet," he barked. "And get that cowpuncher's body somewhere respectable. I suspect there'll be folks along soon to fetch it."

Two men, using all their strength, pulled Darling Annie to her feet. The front of her dress was covered with the blood of the sadly killed wrangler. As she was led past Boone, Annie stopped. "What did you call me?"

Boone stared blankly into her face.

"You called me a lady. You called me...a *lady*, that's what." She lifted her hand, and with an open palm, she patted Boone's whiskered cheek affectionately.

Chapter 16

THERE WAS ONE BIG tent standing tall and colorful in the middle of the field, surrounded by a circling of smaller tents, giving the town of Casper the appearance of a wonderland. Peake and Patterson had their customary band playing marching songs, bleating from the open mouths of trumpets and tubas, accompanied by a steady rolling of drums. It was opening day, and the crowds bulged at the ribboned gates. With all the flair of a Broadway production, Thurgood Patterson, removed his beaver-skinned top hat and hollered over the buzzing of the excited crowd. "Ladies and gentlemen...and children of Casper, step to the ticket booth, purchase your tickets, and...stay all day."

He cut the ribbon, and the crowd pressed through the gates like the water of a burst dam. And in the middle of that crowd, eyes narrow slits and darting, moved Cletus Burke, searching not for Baby Sullivan, but for opportunity. He dodged the throng and the ticket booth and drifted unnoticed between the tents, where he paused to gather his bearings. From here he could see beyond the menagerie of tents to a spot farther out in the fields where the wagons, mostly empty now, were parked in the tall grass. It resembled a coiling snake in the prairie. *That's where the money is*, he thought. *Packed away in a strongbox.*

Burke didn't want the strongbox. He didn't even need it. And he didn't even want all the money. He just wanted enough to grubstake him to Montana, where there would be more money. But for now, he only looked. It promised to be a long day. He turned sharply then and eyed the ticket booth, where the hordes now gathered, a huge pressing of the pack. All this to see a tired, toothless tiger and a man walking on a tightrope. Even the six big elephants appeared asleep on their feet.

Back in New York City, such sideshows as this passed through often. It was where Burke learned how to hawk his skills as a sneak thief. He watched and learned. He'd killed his first man back then when he was barely fifteen. But this he knew; it was the

139

money that mattered. And he knew that the ticket booth was not where it was stored. It was merely where the money collected. In his youth he had learned early that there was always one man who made periodic passes from the ticket booth to another location with a bag filled with cash. This man would take it to a safer location, deposit it into the hands of another person, and then return to the ticket booth and wait for the next transfer.

As a youth he'd been fascinated by the pathetic creatures cowing in the tents—the bearded lady, the man with elephant legs, the tattooed man, the two-headed ram. But the novelty had worn off early. Even the scantily clad showgirls, whom he'd once seen without their faces made up, were nothing but doctored-up hags with fleshy faces. The woman at Peacock's trading post, whom he'd put out of her misery with a bullet, was a queen compared to the worn-out showgirls back then.

Last night, after talking to Peake and Patterson at the hotel, Burke had put together his plan. His horse was at the livery, saddle and bridle within easy reach. He would spend his day preforming the duties of his lie, as railroad agent Flanner Ferguson, looking for a fugitive. But he would keep very close attention to the trips made from the ticket booth to the wagons in the outer field. How often and who the carrier was. He would wait for the third or fourth delivery, not the first. A knife, not a gun. The long-bladed knife he'd taken from Peacock's shelf was fastened to his belt now, hidden beneath the length of his coattail.

He was also ready for the man who had been watching him from a distance. This too was an old trick he knew the circus people employed. Anyone who looked suspicious was dogged by an equally shady sneak. Burke had seen some of his ruffian friends snatched up and pummeled behind a tent for merely looking distrustful. The man watching Burke was also being watched by Burke himself. Burke knew the tricks and laughed at the clumsy attempts at secrecy. Of course he was a weasel-faced character with a bowler hat and a bulge under his coat, either a pistol or a billyjack club.

Small fry, Burke thought.

On the fringes of the circus gate, Buckboard Bob Ottmar's wagon was set up like a portable kitchen. Pots and iron kettles hung over a bed of coals, with biscuits rising in the Dutch oven, beans in another, a large pot of coffee, and strips of dried beef lying on an oil cloth. Folks came, ate, and left their dirty plates and cups in a basin of soapy water. Bob, if nothing else, was a master of keeping five dishes going at the same time, stirring, seasoning, and washing up the plates for the next round of customers with nary a blink of his eye or a hitch in his step. He was a master.

Bob Ottmar was also a man with a memory. Approaching noon he noticed a man who had wandered by several times without buying anything, just looking things over. Later, after his third or fourth pass, the man came up and ordered a cup of coffee. He drank it black out of one of Bob's tin cups, all the while staring off in the direction of the ticket booth. Bob threw a biscuit into a young boy's waiting palm, then glanced back at the man. He looked like most other men there, the showing of a freshly shaven face, square shoulders, intelligent eyes, with one major exception. The ear. Bob looked at the man's ear and saw that a fair amount of the right earlobe was gone, as if it had been cut away, bit away, or shot away.

And then he remembered the Indian girl and her words. This was her man.

They made an early camp near a clear, fast-moving spring. Boone Crowe attended to the horses while Iron Hand put together the makings of a fire. The scalp of Baby Sullivan had been stowed in one of the extra saddlebags by the girl, the blood drying into the same color of the curly orange-red hair of the

141

young killer. She had done this on an impulse, that old Cheyenne custom of sending the hated foe to the afterlife without his hair. She could have done worse, but even now, several hours later, the fierce anger of the moment had simmered, and she rested in the satisfaction that he had paid for his sins, and the devil who had borne away his soul was now feasting on his flesh.

It had simply been more of the killing business. The need for revenge had not disappeared. It all came back to her the instant she saw the murderer standing before her, the hatred boiling up inside of her all over again. She had seen Boone Crowe's look of surprise as she had finished her work and the still bloody carpet of hair dangled from her hand. But his expression didn't mask another look, one of understanding. She had given him back his knife, then returned to the horses, waiting while Crowe conferred with the townsfolk, giving answers to their many questions.

Camping early seemed to her another way of putting space between the killings and another day. As they rode, she watched the way Boone Crowe's brow was set in a deep furrow of thought, his mouth turned down under his big mustache into a frown so severe it almost frightened her. He was a man who hated killing; she'd heard him say it more than once. But he was a man of duty, and it was obvious that his duty now was to avenge the death of his friend, the sergeant. And the woman whom his friend loved, Turtle Woman. Uncle Pea had been Boone Crowe's friend too. So here it was, written on his face.

There was a pain in Boone's gut. He felt as if he'd swallowed a bucket of lead. Under the trees, he spoke softly to the Ghost Horse, telling what he could tell no man. Or woman. The visions of Rose of Sharon that floated through his head gave him a river of shame. She had seen him as a marshal and the burdens it required. But when he walked away from lawing, he had hoped—and she too had probably hoped—that the marshal life was behind them. Most of the details of what happened at Lost River had been left unspoken. But this, he knew, was different. He was interfering into what was army business.

He thought back on days passed. L. P. Quinn was armed. And O'Clery was armed and threating Isabel. Baby Sullivan was on the brink of killing the prostitute. But Pup Murphy? That was nothing but cold-blooded murder. Would he have surrendered if given the chance? Crowe would never know because no chance was given. Even killing the renegade captain at Willow Creek all those years ago had been justified to a certain extent. And how many more had he killed without offering an option of surrender. But what did it matter anyway? They were all dead now. His only reasoning at the time was to eliminate the possibility that they would kill again. Preventative action. Sparing future victims. It was all he had, so he'd hang on to that. He had to remember that Pup Murphy was a killer too.

With the Ghost Horse nudging his shoulder, Crowe took out his Colt and looked at the empty chambers. Four bullets had killed four men. Cletus Burke was the last one. By now the man could be close, or he could be far away. The folks at Duck Trap had not seen him, only Sullivan. No other riders. Both Quinn and O'Clery hinted that Burke had been the one who put desertion into their heads. Even the girl, from her hiding place, had judged him the man giving orders. Boone did not know Burke, but he knew the type. Most truly desperate men were the same, great planners and poor finishers.

West, Boone thought. It was where the younger fugitives he'd chased often headed. He guessed that was where Baby Sullivan would have ended up, had he not ended up dead. But Burke was older. At least from Iron Hand's description of him. Ten years older, maybe more. Even Private Cohen, when he ran into his patrol, had fixed Burke at nearing forty. And that meant something altogether different. Older outlaws usually turned north. They had visions of one last bonanza, and lately, Montana was the bright, shining object of their dreams.

Montana was a considerable piece off, and Boone Crowe did not relish following his man all that long way. He would much prefer to end this business. For a heap of reasons. If Burke gave them the slip, it might take years, and a stroke of luck, for them to ever cross paths again. He imagined finding the deserter in a saloon somewhere. Or simply passing on a trail. It might be winter in the mountain country. Or maybe seeing him from across a campfire. And the recognition would set in, and Crowe would pull out his Colt and kill him. And Burke would never know why.

"Where are we going in the morning?"

The girl's voice surprised Crowe out of his fantasy. She had been watching him, studying him. He was a thinker, she knew. A deeply private and mysterious man. And just now she was sure his mind was turning like a millwheel.

"I'm trying to figure the man out," he said. "What he'd do. Where he'd go from where he was."

"And?"

"Army life ain't no carnival. Especially at a prairie fort like Laramie. The monotony alone works hard to kill you. Soldiers desert fairly regularly. They just don't go on a killing spree."

He was silent again, and she let him think.

"They could have bargained with your uncle for horses and supplies, and Peacock would have likely welcomed the trade. My guess is they had murder on their minds from the beginning."

Iron Hand nodded. "Baby Sullivan was in a town when we found him. So were the first two. And Quinn said O'Clery was going to Cheyenne. Are you thinking that's where Burke might be? In a town somewhere?"

"Or heading there." He stood from the campfire and strolled to a small knoll where he could see the Laramie Mountain range to the south. And much farther, to the northwest, he glimpsed the distant peaks of the Bighorns. Just once he would like to enjoy this beautiful view without having murder on his mind. Burke's and his own.

The girl, not satisfied to be left alone, followed him to the top of the hill.

Without looking at her, he said, "Casper's the next town

of any size. It's not a hole-in-the-wall like Duck Trap. Bob said something about a circus. I'm up for goin there next."

"I've never seen a circus."

Crowe looked down at the dog standing at her feet and then at her soft features. *Hell,* he thought. *She's just a kid.* "I don't recollect I have either," he said. "Not out here anyway."

They took it slow, as not to wear out the only horse they had. Bright Cohen and Henry Mussel rode double off and on, then they'd walk to rest the critter. They had considered their options and agreed to do nothing would produce like results. They had to move, even if they had no plan beyond their hunches.

"I sure can't go back to the fort. They'd hang me for sure," Cohen reasoned. "Since I'm likely figured dead, I mays well stay that way."

They had managed ten miles, moving roughly northeast, when Henry Mussel pointed to the sky. "Meat eaters," he said, indicating a band of vultures circling in a frenzy half a mile away. By the time they reached the scene of the carnage, the stench hit their nostrils. Lying on the ground was an outstretched body, bloated nearly black, with four buzzards perched around it, their ugly beaks tearing at the flesh.

Cohen threw a rock, and the birds retreated a few yards, shrieking angrily. More vultures circled low above them. Covering Cohen's nose and mouth with a scarf, he edged closer. Even in this state, he could see where a single bullet had made a canyon of his skull, from the top of his nose to the crown of his red hair. It was O'Clery; Cohen knew him instantly. He'd been stripped of his weapons, and even though he wore a checkered shirt, torn to tatters now by the carrion eaters, he still wore the familiar boots and leggings of an infantryman.

Bright Cohen backed away, fighting off a wave of nausea.

Henry Mussel, meantime, searched the area for signs, but

145

only the faintest of horse prints showed in the sand, too weather-faded to read. Together they moved upwind of the body, leaving the buzzards to their work. "I ain't gettin close to that again. Sides, he ain't worth buryin anyway."

"Maybe Straw Dog?"

"Or Boone Crowe," Cohen said. "It's hard to reckon. Either way, dead is dead."

Henry Mussel put his face to the direction they had been traveling. "More miles."

"Suits me. I ain't fond of this place. Sides, it'll be light for another couple hours."

They watered the horse at the pool and then continued on, angling more north now, away from O'Clery and far from Fort Laramie.

It was all plotted out. In the middle of the day Cletus Burke retired to the livery stable and napped on a pile of straw. He had watched the routine of collecting the money from the ticket booth every hour and the transfer of it to one of the wagons on the outer circle. This was done by the same man every time, a squat dumpling with spectacles resting on a narrow, bladed nose and a collar too tight for his neck, giving his face the look of a red beet.

This little man, Burke believed, could be squashed like a bug. But he also knew that the man Decius, whom the circus owners had put to shadowing him, would be ever-present, lurking about. If he intended to be stealthy, the oaf had done a poor job of it. Burke had his army pistol, but this was a job for a knife, and he had gotten his hands on a beauty without much effort. He had been a butcher in New York City, but a master thief also. It was an effective skill to possess in a cutthroat district like Five Points.

Outside he could hear the constant rattle and rumble of the circus, the bleating of the sideshow men hawking their attractions. And the steady roar of the crowd. It was a far cry from the desolation of Fort Laramie, where the sound of the wind was the only hope of blotting out the noise of the bugle and the barking of that damn Sergeant Tunneson, shouting orders.

Burke smiled, thinking about it. *That voice has been buggered out. Along with that Crow bitch of his.* He lay in the straw, revisiting the whole scene. It was blood in his nostrils again, and it seemed as if he could bring the whole thing back at will. He lifted the knife, which laid beside him, and drawing it up close to his face, he kissed the blade. "We are back in business," he said.

The sun appeared to be moving fast, and he watched the shadows creep across the stable walls. Getting up, Burke moved to the horse trough and plunged his head into the water. He then scrubbed at his face, and finally ran his fingers through his thick hair, drawing it back tight against his head. Hat back on, knife stowed out of sight, he saddled his horse and casually wandered between the tents. He found a place in a clump of bushes where several other horses were tied, and he fastened his mount with a loose loop for easy escape. He then sauntered toward the chuck wagon, where the friendly cook had sold his wares. He was hungry now, and he wanted a full belly for the work ahead to be done.

Burke had considered once just robbing this chuck wagon cook, but the man wore his pistol in a fashion that fairly dared action. A cookie with a deadeye for trouble. Burke thought better of it. At the sight of his approach, Buckboard Bob poured a cup of fresh coffee and held it out to him.

"Obliged," Burke said.

"Are you in for a plate of beef and beans? I'm about to fold up fer the night, and I got leftovers."

"Why, that's mighty accommodating of you, partner."

"I'm not one to waste. But it's gettin that time for me to pull up stakes. I got tracks to make."

"Where's that?"

"North, I reckon," Bob said.

"Ha. Me too. Or, well...I thought about it anyway."

147

"You know the country?"

"Not much."

Bob Ottmar said no more, busying himself with wrapping things up. He had kettles to clean and plates to wash.

After a while Burke asked, "What is up north? I'm from back east, so I'm fresh off the train."

"Come in from Cheyenne, did ya?"

"Yes. Yes. Sure."

Bob pulled down a kettle from its hook. "Well, if ya went far enough north, you'd likely see one of them polar bears." He gave himself a chuckle. "Otherwise, it's Fort Tillman. That's where I'm headed. And then there's Buffalo. Beyond that you got the silver country of Montana. Silver and copper. Cattle too. As many or more than we got here."

"You don't say." Burke finished the beef and beans and handed back the plate. "You're a fine gentleman. I thank ye kindly." Buckboard Bob said good night and watched the man drift off into the noise and darkness of the crowd.

The mass moved toward one of the big tents where a man with a horn was bellowing out a welcome. *Find a seat and get ready for the show of a lifetime.* Burke let the throng press against him, pushing toward the wide open tent flaps, but then, at the last minute, he edged to the side and away. He was in the shadows now, waiting for the people to enter the big top and settle in for the performance. The little beetle of a man would be collecting the money from the ticket booth any minute now, so he moved away to watch close. He looked over his shoulder and scanned the darkness for Decius but saw no sign of him. Not yet, but he suspected Decius was close.

Then, as if as perfectly printed on a theater program, the little man with the sharp nose weaseled between the smaller tents and emerged at the backdoor of the ticket booth. Looking right and left, he knocked, and instantly the door opened. Burke waited and in another minute the little man reappeared, holding a canvas money bag. With another look around, he shoved the bag under his coat flap and once again disappeared among the small tents.

But Burke knew the drill and waited as the moneyman reemerged and began his trek across the field to the office wagon. He never made it. Burke, like the snake he was, had stationed himself in the tall sawgrass. At just the right moment, he stood, nearly killing the little man with fright. A quick blow to the man's head with the butt end of Burke's knife, and the job was done. Pulling the canvas bag from under the coat, Burke felt the heft of it and smiled.

The night seemed to hang on a thread; then from the big top the crowd erupted in cheers. Burke saw the unmistakable form of Decius. He resembled a grizzly bear staring off into the night. He appeared to be focusing on Burke, and unfortunately the circus thug stood in the path of Burke's escape, his horse tied to the branches just a few feet away. At Burke's feet the little moneyman groaned. He was regaining himself, and Burke knew it was time to get it done. Pulling the revolver from its holster, he started a slow walk toward the big man.

At fifty paces he stopped and waited. They could see each other clearly now, and even in the shadowy night, their eyes glistened under the moonlight. Burke continued to wait, neither man moving. Then, suddenly, from under the big tent, a cannon roared as the human cannon ball was launched into the air, heading toward a net fifty feet beyond. It was a repeat of the performance Burke had witnessed that afternoon. It was not a cannon, but rather a concocted catapult that launched the man into the air. A real cannon was blown simultaneously from an old military piece for dramatic effect. The crowd too exploded with a frenzy of thunderous cheers, and Burke's pistol also blasted, covered by the cannon's noise. A well-aimed bullet hit Decius' just below his chin and straightened the big man up. Decius' hands started upward to his throat, but they fell limply, and he dropped like a sack of oats into the grass.

Burke laughed as he stared down at the silly circus guard. "Ye ain't so pretty now, are ye?" he said. "What say we go for a little ride?" Bent on escape, he quickly stowed the money into his saddlebag. Then taking one of the other horses tied to the bushes, he led it to where the dead Decius lay. He was a bear-sized oaf, but Burke managed to hoist the body onto the horse, even while the animal protested. Grabbing the reins, he jerked the horse's head. "Stop fretting," he told the animal. "It'll only be a short ride."

Into the night he rode, leading the other horse and its burden out of Casper and away from the fading chaos of the hollering circus crowd. The night was turning colder, but it felt good against his face as he galloped away, his horse rested and ready for a Montana-bound run. Two miles into the prairie Burke, not missing a stride, edged up close to the other mount. He grabbed the dead man by his wooly vest and pulled him from the saddle and onto the ground. "Sweet dreams, ye damn fool." He laughed over his shoulder as he rode toward the yellow circle of moon.

Chapter 17

PEAKE AND PATTERSON'S LITTLE moneyman, whose name was Fennimore Tibbs, sat on a chair in the circus's wagon office, a linsey-woolsey bandage around his head. It was morning, but he had not slept, nor had either Amos Peake or Thurgood Patterson. They had lost the revenue of an entire afternoon's profits, and the likely thief was long gone. R. D. Decius was missing also, and the blame showed clearly on him. *Who else?* the two men wondered. It was an inside job, and only Decius knew the routine of Tibbs.

They had grilled the little man to tears, but all they could get from him, in a shaky voice, was, *I got it from behind. Never saw a thing.* It was only now, after affixing the blame on Decius that they remembered they still had a circus to run. "We'll just have to change things up," Peake said. "No more collecting alone. Thurgood, either you or myself have to be there every time the switch is made." He shook his head. "But if I ever lay eyes on Decius again, I'll feed him to that damn tiger."

"The show must go on," Patterson offered, shoulders sagging.

"May I get some rest now, sir?" Tibbs begged, his throat tight.

Both men looked at him. His spectacles were ajar, and a slight swelling was forming under his right eye. "Rest?" bellowed Peake. "You're lucky you still have a job. I've a notion to leave you in this godforsaken place. One more slipup and you'll be working the backend of the elephants."

Daylight was nearly spent by the time Boone Crowe and Iron Hand entered Casper from the east. But even in the gloaming, the big, brightly painted circus tent was still visible against the crimson sky. They reined in and took in the site. The girl's eyes were transfixed. "It must be a big family to need a tipi that big." Crowe looked at her but saw a gleam in her eye. They had come through some rough country, but looking at her now, as she held the dog against her in the saddle, he felt charmed by her innocent comments.

As they rode through the darkened street, lamplight and noise spilled out from several saloons. Farther on, where the circus stretched out, there was more noise. Indistinguishable words were being blurted from some kind of speaking tube, followed by cheers and laughter from the assembled crowd in the big top tent. "Are we staying here tonight?" Iron Hand asked.

"Depends. If Burke is here, we can end this business and go home."

The word *home* stuck in the girl's head. She had no home. A gloom edged into her mind.

"But if he's not here..." He didn't finish his thought. If Burke wasn't in Casper, or never had been, then their trail had gone cold.

Iron Hand leaned forward and let the dog lick her face. *Margot. You are all I have,* she thought.

The two searchers were a sight themselves. A tattered old man and an Indian girl, with a string of horses on a lead rope. They rode past the livery stable, then turned back and dismounted. Boone gave out a halloo and the boy, Low, scrambled out through the big open door. "Whoa, mister," he said, his eyes wide. "That's quite a string you got there. Fear I'll have to put 'em in the far back. We're plumb full up in the stable cuz of the circus and all."

"You got a corral back there?"

"Corral and a lean-to big enough for horses. Water too. Pa had to add it on some piece back."

"Put these four that's on a lead back there. These two, the ones we're on, I want handy. Understand?"

The boy gave a salute, finally turning his eye to the girl. "The show is still goin on if that's where yer fixin to go. I went yesterday and saw a fellow with legs the size of an elephant's. And there was a man with tattoos from his toes to the top of his head. Gave me a wink, he did. There was a woman too, with a beard down to here." He touched a place on his chest.

152

"You got a sheriff around?"

"Sure 'nough. But he's plenty busy, accounta the robbery."

Boone Crowe had seen an open bag of oats, and he reached in and fetched a handful for the Ghost Horse. "What robbery?"

"One of the fellows that works for the circus. Well, he used to work for the circus. He got plumb away with some of the ticket money. Lit out last night. Not till he brained the fella. The one who counts that loot. I seen him walkin around today with a bandage around his head."

"How do you know all this?"

"Look, mister. I got ears. And these ears listen."

Boone looked at the girl, then back to the boy. "Speakin of ears. You seen a man with a shot-off ear? Shot off or chewed off."

"Him. Oh, yeah. The bounty hunter. He was here."

Iron Hand moved in close now, standing at Crowe's side. "He *was* here?" she questioned.

"Left last night."

"Did he say where? Where he was going?" The girl had moved so close the boy could see her face clearly.

"You're a Indian, ain't you?"

Iron Hand ignored his remark and repeated her question.

Low studied her, fascinated more by her beauty than her anger. "Not to me, he didn't."

"The man is no bounty hunter," she spat. "He is a murderer."

"A...murderer?" the boy gasped. "Who'd he—"

"Never mind," Boone said finally. "Tell me what he looked like. Besides the ear."

"Well, he was dressed up kinda funny for a bounty hunter. He had a checked shirt and a flop hat. But his horse was a dandy. Speckled on the rump. Came in pretty worn out, but I took good care of him and he was fit to run again."

Boone blew out a long sigh. "And you say he left last night?"

"Bout this same time. He come in all cheerful. Like he was happy to be shed of this place."

Boone turned to Iron Hand, and they shared a penetrating

stare. "He's got a day on us. But we've gotta let our critters rest a bit. Besides, we got no trail in the dark. But I'm still bettin on north. Let's go see if we can dig up more information. Someone must have seen him."

"Ya know, mister, you might check down by the circus. There's a fella with one of them outdoor kitchens. He was makin a wagon load of money, I reckon, cause he was always dishin it out. And, that other fella, the one you're lookin for, every time I wandered down that way, they was talkin up a heap, like they was old pals."

Crowe felt the girl tense. Margot, at her feet, looked up into her face. Iron Hand picked her up and turned toward the door. "How far is that wagon of his?"

"Can't miss it. Even in the dark. He got about three lanterns hangin from pegs. Straight down the street and to yer right."

Boone Crowe caught up to Iron Hand, who had already taken off, and they set a steady stride together, the three lanterns already within sight, yellow beacons in the night.

Out of the night, into the day, and now approaching night again, Cletus Burke rode, stopping only to rest and water his horse several times, his watchful eyes forever on the back trail. But only now did he feel comfortable stopping for the night. *If someone was following me,* he reasoned, *they would have shown themselves by now.* It was time to give his horse a real rest and himself too. He found a place where he could see in all directions and built a campfire. He'd managed to pilfer food and utensils and now heated a can of pemmican and bannock.

Eating hurriedly, Burke dug out the circus moneybag with anticipation and set it before him on the ground. The bills and coins had been thrown in loosely, but drawing out a handful he gasped. They were small denominations, but they were plentiful, so ignoring the coins, he counted out nearly five hundred dollars. And there was more. *I'm rich,* he thought. *There's probably that much and more in the bag. Plus the silver. A damn fortune.* Stretching under a blanket on the ground, he used the moneybag for a pillow.

Under the stars Burke's mind sifted a hundred thoughts, all of them with happy endings.

Bright Cohen's prediction about his fabricated death, and how it was received by Captain Gillespie, was a true one. When Private Martin Cochran told his fable about how he and Cohen were trapped and how he saw with his own two eyes his friend falling from his horse with at least three arrows in him, the captain did exactly what Cohen guessed he would do—he shrugged.

"Are you in the mood to take a patrol out and retrieve his body?"

"Not exactly, sir."

"Fine then. Let the red devils have him."

"Yessir."

But as ex-private Bright Cohen watched Henry Mussel kindling a fire, he would not know any of this for a number of years, long after he'd moved on with his life. It was today, though, still riding double, when they came across a second dead body, this one belonging to L. P. Quinn, dead, though still in a sitting position. But Quinn's horse stood nearby when they arrived.

"This one here's Quinn," Cohen said. "You recognize him?"

Henry Mussel shook his head. "Knocked out. Only saw boy who shot me."

"Well, I know him. And I know he was one of 'em. But look at him now. Slumped over, still sittin on his cowardly ass bone. That's two down. Critters haven't gotten to him yet, though."

"Two horses now," Henry said.

"And whoever sent him to hell left his pistol there in the sand. Three bullets in his belt. Hell, they just might be all we need tomorrow if we can sneak up on a ram or something."

The night was turning chilly, so the two men sat around the

flames of the fire and pondered over the dead Quinn. "Who do you reckon? Straw Dog? Or old Marshal Crowe?"

Henry Mussel shrugged. "Great circle found him. Death comes to the dead."

Cohen considered this and decided it made more sense than it sounded. Sooner or later, death comes for us all, but for the deadly, probably sooner. And he was okay with that because the world was shed of one more madman.

The circus closed for the night, and Boone Crowe, Iron Hand, and Buckboard Bob Ottmar sat on barrels and ate the leftover beef and beans of Bob's busy day. Margot, black and shiny, tail striking the ground in cheerful rhythm, worried the last meat off of a bone.

"She's taken to you," Bob said to Iron Hand. "She seems a might happier in yer company."

"We don't have the fixins you do, but she likes the girl's devotion," Boone said. "And what dog wouldn't?"

The subject of Cletus Burke had been covered at length, and their conclusions were all the same. It wasn't the bodyguard who'd stolen the money, as the circus bosses believed. This was the desperate move of the deserter.

"And you think he's going to Montana?"

Bob nodded. "He let that slip a time or two. I figured it was yer man, what with the ear and all. But he was plumb excited, like he had this big plan. And he was just bustin to tell somebody about it."

"Well," Crowe said, "you do have that sweet, innocent face. If you can get past that croaky voice of yers."

"What do you think?" Bob said, looking at Iron Hand. "Do I have a sweet, innocent face?"

She flashed a rare smile. "Very sweet."

"Enough flattery," Bob laughed. "Boone. What's the plan?"

"Well, all the talks about Butte these days. Copper now, on top of silver. A man like Burke has a nose for riches. And it's a place he could likely get lost."

"So. It's off to Butte then?"

Crowe nodded. "At first light."

"I've been there, Boone. And," he said, nodding to Iron Hand, "it's a rough and tumble place. It's no place for a young girl."

Iron Hand's smile vanished, and her eyes darted to Boone Crowe.

Bob went on. "I'm heading in the direction of Ft. Tillman. I'd be happy to fetch her along with me."

The girl stood, arms across her chest.

The old marshal tipped his head toward Buckboard Bob. "The girl has spoken." A faint smile flickered under his big mustache.

"No need to get yer feathers ruffled, lady. It was just a thought. But that just means you best find yer man *before* you get to Butte. Long before."

Chapter 18

THE HORSE WAS STANDING with reins hanging down when Boone Crowe and Iron Hand saw its silhouette against the dawn light. Their first thought was that they'd already found their man, but on closer inspection, they found the dead body of Decius sprawled in the tall grass nearby. The man's neck was opened up by a bullet, but the blood was black now, and the look on his face gave off the unexpected shock of death. They dismounted and searched the area for a sign, but there was little of it. Only the tracks of a second horse. But no sign of struggle. And no money sacks.

Crowe stood, facing north, the retreating tracks weaving in that direction. "Well, that's a sure bet."

They remounted and followed the trail for the rest of the day. By sundown they came upon Burke's old campfire, burnt out and scattered, but not scattered enough.

"We'll camp here. So long as we can keep a day between us, we'll catch him sooner or later. Hopefully sooner. He's feeling relaxed, by the looks of things."

The girl made her bed without a further word and then wandered into the darkness for a while, returning with a piece of paper money. She held it out to Crowe. "It was stuck in the bushes."

Crowe took it. "This must be where he counted it. And this one got away." He gave it back to her. "Add it to your little money box."

The fire was made and the supper fixings put together. Afterward Crowe finished a cigar he'd tried to finish for two days. Blowing smoke into the ever-chilling wind, he studied the girl, who stared into the fire. "I've been admiring that deer skin poncho you're wearing. Those flowers drawn on there are pleasant to look at. Especially on this ride."

"My aunt made it for me. Uncle Pea shot the deer, and she tanned it. Then drew the flowers. She gave it to me when I returned from the east. It was meant to cheer me."

"Did it?"

"It helped. Now it is just something to remember the bad that happened to them."

Boone was sorry he'd mentioned it. He stared into the night sky, hoping to find a future hidden out there. But he knew how things worked in these times. He chewed on his cigar, aiming the smoke at stars that seemed distant and unhearing. Finally he said, with more wish than truth, "Maybe they'll cheer you again. Someday.

The girl looked at him but made no answer.

The woman in the little shop looked up from the book she was reading when the man entered. Her little store was always open, day or night, but few ever walked through her doors after dark. She sized him up—flop hat, checked shirt, high-top army boots, and the start of a new beard. Always on the lookout for trouble, she saw none in this man's face. His quick smile betrayed any mistrust she might see in him.

"You're late out," she said.

"I am in full agreement, my fine lady," Burke said. "But my tired eyes saw ye lantern light, and it was like a beacon on the sea."

She laughed. "Well, ain't you the poet."

"Cattle buyer, I'm afraid. The beacon is where my poetics ends. What me sees mostly is the back end of cows."

"You don't look like a drover."

"No ma'am, a buyer, as I said. On me way back to Montana. Me cows have been bought and will be shipped by rail."

The woman's shop was dimly lit and carried all manner of items, some hanging from pegs, others piled on the counter and on shelves. She had a few tables scattered about with mostly used items, from clothes, farm tools, leather goods, and the occasional firearm. An assortment of canned goods too found their place on a shelf, as well as a cracker barrel and a jar of pickles in brine.

"This place have a name?" he asked.

"Home," she answered good-naturedly. She saw him looking through the window into the darkness. "We're just here. There's me, the grain storage structure across the street, and that hotel, as it has been referred. The owner calls it Paradise, but those who've spent the night there call it Flea-Bite Hotel."

"Hmm. What about a drink?"

"He sells it. Over there. Can't vouch for its drinkability."

Burke nodded. "I've had all kinds," he said absently.

He was holding up something, inspecting it, but the woman couldn't see it for the dim interior.

"Do you do trades?" he asked.

"That's the bulk of my business, mister. Ain't nobody got any real money around here. Includin the farmers. So, when they need something, it's pretty much a trade. I ain't got no money either."

"That's a hardship I understand. I just spent my fortune on cattle, for better or for worse. Such is the business."

In the woman's mind the man had stayed too long. So she quietly moved to where she'd left her book on the counter. Reaching beneath, she retrieved her equalizer, a double-barreled shotgun. She laid it down quietly so that it was within quick reach, with the twin yawning barrels pointing outward. Her floor still carried the torn up pellet marks from an incident two years before. *This fella's friendliness is a might too friendly,* she thought. *I know cattle buyers, and he ain't one, far as I can tell.* From mere survival, she knew that most folks came in with something on their mind, bought it or traded for it, and skedaddled. *This fella's got a whole different story, and he ain't tellin it,* she reasoned.

"Hard times then, huh?"

"Ain't seen no other," she said.

When Burke turned he saw the shotgun lying on the counter, aimed directly at him, something he hadn't seen when he came

161

in. He smiled. *Time to make a trade,* he thought. *There's better ways to die than by the hand of a prairie-hardened woman.*

"Let's talk turkey, ma'am."

Straw Dog had seen the bodies of O'Clery and Quinn too, hours before Cohen and Henry Mussel stumbled on them. But he had not disturbed them, knowing to do so would be bad medicine. If he had killed them himself, it would have been a different matter. But here, he knew, had been the work of the crow man. The old marshal. But looking at the markings left by the copse of trees, Straw Dog found the second pair of prints, moccasin prints, and small. The girl. The one Henry Mussel spoke of. She was not killed at the trading post as the younger Indian had believed. And she wasn't killed here either. It could mean only one thing. She is with the crow man.

Leaning against his horse's rump, patting it affectionately, he considered all things as they were laid before him. The crow man was on a trail of blood. And where he went dead men were left. He was Tunneson's friend too, so he was seeking his own revenge. The Indian scout closed his eyes, and then, turning south, he saw a picture of the future. He would chase the deserters no more. Let the crow man have them.

Mounting, he turned into a distance he knew well. *There are other matters,* he said to himself, and with heels to his horse, he rode away.

They were up before daylight, having slept only lightly. They were getting close and felt it. A familiar rage built in Boone Crowe again. He had dreamt of phantoms and gunfire in the thick, smoke-laden trees of The Wilderness, back in the war— the war that was forever there, never having left him. Waking with a start, he lay under his bedroll, sweating. The girl was also sleeping fitfully. She had cried out once, earlier in the night. *We're bound by revenge,* he thought. *And I'm not teaching her anything about the limits of law. And how can I, when I am acting outside the law myself?*

It was the land, he knew, that always brought him back to a quiet place. Wyoming was fair as a beautiful woman, and the tall grass and prairie sage that stretched before him now were like a balm to his troubled mind. *If all the world was gone,* he thought, *Lord, please save Wyoming for me.* In the far distance he saw the white heads of curious pronghorns lift, their searching eyes watching them. Coyotes too, slinking through the brush, was as much a part of him as the sky and its rain. He saw Iron Hand looking around too, and he wondered what she might be thinking.

The still visible trail spoke volumes about the reasoning of Cletus Burke. Even with somewhat of a background in army maneuvering, the man was showing no clear sense in covering his tracks. It could only mean one thing, he felt safe that no posse from Casper pursued him. Either that, or he was just plain stupid. No matter which, he might as well be leaving signposts telling where he was going. All the better. Once the man was in his grave, his future, unknowing victims could breathe a sigh of relief.

By mid-afternoon Boone Crowe and Iron Hand saw three buildings in the distance, surrounded by nothing but open prairie, standing like lonesome sentinels in the October sun. Farther, where the sky blended into infinity, layers of black clouds were gathering.

"That's weather we don't need," Boone said.

"Maybe he's there, in that town."

"It's possible. We best be on guard."

Iron Hand touched Baby Sullivan's .44 she had tucked against her leg and the saddle horn. Crowe too removed the thong from his Colt's hammer.

A woman stood on the packed dirt in front of a store, watching them ride in, as if she'd been expecting them. The look on her face was a look Crowe knew all too well, that expression of tragic disbelief, usually after something bad has happened.

"If you're the law, you're too late," the woman said.

Iron Hand was looking around, sizing up the little town. Across the street from where the woman was standing, she noticed a bustle of men milling in the open doorway of a saloon. Crowe saw it too, but dismounting he moved to the woman.

"Unprovoked," the woman said.

"A shooting?"

"A killing."

"Who?"

"Friendly Bill Bitters. Owner of the Black Diamond there. His only crime was the bad whisky he peddled. But Friendly Bill wouldn't squash a spider." She wiped at her troubled face with a hankie.

"Who?"

"Drifter. Claimed to be a cattle buyer, but I saw through that."

"Was he wearing any army clothes?"

The woman motioned to the door. "Come inside. I'll show you what he traded to me."

Crowe and the girl followed her inside and watched as the woman lifted an army issue belt and holster, with the bright gold US stamped on the buckle. "He came in wearing this. Traded me for an older one, plain brown leather. He asked about the saloon, and I told him the whisky was bad and the beer warm." She shook her head. "I only told him that, hopin he'd just saddle up and ride out. Friendly Bill's beer ain't warm at all. He's got ice under a pile of straw in his cellar."

"What's yer name?"

"Selena. This here's my shop. What you see is what you get. What Friendly had is what you get too...and now he's gone."

"Man have a shot-off ear?"

"Hard to miss, that ear."

"Cletus Burke," Iron Hand hissed.

Boone studied the woman, realizing she had to be tough to set roots down in a scratch of a town like this and stay. She was not old or young, the streaks of gray in her otherwise brown hair were premature, but the old marshal could easily see the prettiness that had once resided there. But this business with Bill Bitters had clearly taken something out of her.

"How long ago?"

"I heard the gunshot around midnight. I was sitting in my chair, dozing off. I don't sleep much."

"And then he rode out?"

"Right after. Go...go on over and talk to Hinkle. He was there and saw the whole thing. He's over there now."

Hinkle too was shaken. When Boone spoke to him, he was nearly in tears, telling how the man kept drinking and getting drunker by the minute. "Old Friendly Bill said it was closing time, and the bastard pulled out his pistol and said, plain as day, he said, 'It's closing time for you too,' and he shot old Bill through the heart."

Iron Hand found Crowe's eyes and saw the fire burning there.

"I feared fer myself, I did," Hinkle said. "I froze. Like a hunk of rock. And he did...he pointed his pistol straight at me. Then he laughed. Picked up a bottle of whisky, threw it at Bill's mirror, turnin it to shards. Then he laughed again, like a madman. I closed my eyes. When I opened them, he was gone, and I heard his horse riding out. Leaving hell for his trouble."

Boone Crowe could see the dead man's boots sticking out from behind the bar. "Git this man buried. He ain't going to bury himself," he said.

Chapter 19

CLETUS BURKE SLEPT IN the saddle until he fell off. Even the impact of hitting the ground did little to stir him from his drunken stupor. He rolled onto his back and snored, momentarily spooking his horse. It took a pestering cluster of deer flies to finally wake him. His head felt like an anvil, with a burly blacksmith standing over him swinging a hammer. Lying there, forcing his eyes open, he saw the sky, black with clouds looming above him. The first sloppy raindrops splashed against his face. Within minutes he was drenched and struggling to find shelter. He wedged himself under a dead, fallen tree and moaned in misery.

He woke again an hour later to see the ground covered in white snow and the temperature dropping. *This won't do*, he thought. Out of one eye he spied his horse fifty yards away with a layer of snow dusting its flanks. *How the hell am I going to get to Montana in a mess like this?* He cursed himself for last night. It was that old bloodlust again. Even drunk, he knew what he was doing. He just couldn't help himself. It had been that way at the trading post. And with Tunneson. Killing was better than laying with a woman, he felt, his face finally putting on a ghoulish smile.

But what to do now? The wind was picking up too. Burke lowered his head in despair. He couldn't go back to the town. And what lay ahead he did not know. It would be dark in a few hours. Wobbling to his horse, he drew up the reins and pulled himself into the wet saddle. Finding north was not easy with the steady falling snow and the gray sky, he gave the horse its head, shivering in the wind-whipped storm.

Baby Sullivan crept into Burke's mind, and he wondered what had become of him. It was another of Burke's big mistakes, not shooting the little halfwit. He dreamt for a while just how he might have done it, letting his mind work up the bloody details of various methods. Back at Five Points, he remembered the rush of swinging his battle axe, and the blood that covered him in the heat of the fights. The thought warmed him as he rode.

Iron Hand had stopped, dismounted, and pulled her deerskin robe from her bedding, and remounting, she draped it over her shoulders. She put Margot in front of her on the saddle, both of them sharing each other's meager warmth. The dog, uncomplaining, licked her hand. Crowe too had drawn a wool vest from his tack and put it on, raising the collar against the wind. They were facing open country—country he knew—and couldn't recall any kind of natural shelter, save a rocky outcropping where a ravine had been cut into the steppe by a washout years back. But that was ten miles or more and not in a straight line from here. But the snow had wiped out Burke's tracks, so it was a blind trek anyway.

Boone Crowe had seen worse, had survived worse. After he had learned of Little Feet being sent to Florida on a prison train, he'd quit the scouting job and fled to the mountains to clear his mind. He wintered with the Nez Perce. It was the year before they were chased off their homeland, chased to their defeat by General Howard. A gentle people, he knew, who shared their tipis, food, and wisdom with him. Their winter had been like this, he remembered. The blunder of Custer had set the army, and the whole world it seemed, on the hunt for Indians, peaceable or not.

But in the deepest of snow, he fought his way out of his sadness. Trying to find Little Feet in a place so far away would be futile, but he remembered everything about her, and now traveling with this young woman, brought all the memories back. *A thousand what-ifs,* he thought. How his life would have been different. And then, four years ago, it was the same story all over again with Eva where she laid at Dead Woman Creek. He thought his well was dry after that, until Rose of Sharon came into his life, unexpected as this snowstorm.

"Look!" It was Iron Hand, pointing. Putting her heels to her horse, she sprinted to a fallen tree off to the right.

Crowe followed and watched as the girl dismounted. "Look," she said again. "He's been here."

Sure enough, the girl had seen where the ground under the dead tree had been scraped with boot heels, untouched by the snow from the shelter of the log.

"It might not be him," Boone said, pulling his hat tighter against the wind.

"It's him. This place is troubled by his evil spirit. Can't you feel it?"

"How long ago do you think?"

"I don't know such things. Only that it is him."

Boone Crowe touched the girl on her arm. "Listen. You don't want to hear this, but we can't go on. This storm is getting worse."

"No," she shrieked. "He's out there. We have to go. Now." She started back to her horse, but Boone managed to seize her reins.

"Isabel, you've gotta listen. This weather is a killer. This fallen tree isn't much, but it's all we've got. We have to get inside and stay out of the wind."

She grabbed for the reins, but Crowe pulled them back. Her rage finally turned to tears. "He...he killed my family. He..." Her sobs were carried off by the wind. Finally her shoulders slumped and she hung her head. "What...about the horses?"

"You get inside. I hate to say it, but the horses will have to do their best without us."

Iron Hand was still crying when she and the dog crawled under the shelter of the fallen tree. Boone Crowe took one final glance at the horses, then pressed himself in beside the girl. Putting his arm around her, he pulled her close to share their warmth.

It was the horse that found the shelter of the old abandoned barn, half-collapsed from disuse and years of weather. Cletus Burke, wet and frozen, opened his eyes in surprise, just inside the gaping door, smelling the scent of old wood and long-rotted hay. He slid off his horse and fell like a dead man onto the ancient dust of the barn floor. It took a long time for his senses to revive, but after a time, shivering, he put together decayed pieces of wood and straw and constructed a fire. And there, for long hours, he sat warming himself back to life, periodically adding fuel to the small blaze.

Waiting for the fire to take hold, he removed the saddle from the horse and used the saddle blanket to rub down the animal as best he could. The horse was all he had, and he would need it if he hoped to reach his destination. Sometime in the night the wind laid down, and he woke to the silence of it. Standing at the barn door and staring into the gray dawn, he saw that the snow had stopped, replaced again by an icy rain. Now he spotted another building fifty yards off, smaller but in the same abandoned and windowless condition. A long forsaken farm, he reasoned. Gone bust and moved on.

Burke saw something else too. Two riders on the crest of a rise, leading a string of horses. They were coming this way, two ghosts in the morning mist. *More refugees from the storm*, he figured. He rummaged through his tack where he'd scattered it the night before until he found his pistol and holster and strapped it back on. This wide open country was suddenly getting a bit overpopulated. Getting out of Casper had suited him fine, but now this. *What's their business?* he wondered and waited.

Boone Crowe and Iron Hand too had felt the storm pass over and crawled from their shelter. Then they searched for the horses. The critters had bunched up, partly in confusion and partly to create a five-horse shelter against the wind so the riders took to rubbing them down. A horse can survive a cold night simply by burning their own fat, but they would need fuel soon to replace what they burned. The rain was driving off the snow, so the grass was easy to find again.

Forfeiting their own breakfast, the two fugitive hunters rode through the rest of the night until the distant, gray sun put a pair of shadows on the land—two old forsaken buildings. And smoke, shifting through breaks in the roof. They reined in and studied the situation.

"Did he ever see you? At the trading post?"

Iron Hand shook her head. "He came once with the sergeant. But Uncle Pea hid me then too. There was something about this man my uncle did not like."

"Well, I don't reckon he's ever seen me either. We need to use that to our advantage best we can. At least to get close." He rubbed at the whiskers on his chin. "But he's dangerous."

Back at the little town where Friendly Bill Bitters was killed, Iron Hand had gone back into Selena's shop, and with the dollar she'd found in the bushes, she bought the cavalry holster that Burke had traded away. Pilfering through the arsenal they had collected from the men they had killed, she took a Colt and shoved it into the army holster. She was ready.

With caution, they pushed their horses forward.

Inside the barn Burke watched. *This is an odd pair,* he thought. An old man and a young Indian woman. The old man might be an Indian too but likely not. He checked his revolver and then looked around the barn for a place to hide. Hanging from a nail on the wall was an old sickle with a rusty blade, left behind just like the barn and the house to rot with the ages. He smiled, his old love for butchery returning. He picked it up with relish.

Outside the horses approached. "Hello!" Boone hollered. No answer.

They dismounted. "Keep back while I check the barn. But watch the back in case he makes a run for it. No deals. Just kill him."

Iron Hand placed Margot at her feet and drew her pistol. She watched as Boone, his own pistol in hand, stepped through the barn door. The fire in the center of the floor still issued a gray smoke, filling the barn with its haze. "I know yer in here, Cletus Burke. And I am here to kill you."

Then, out of the haze came the deserter, swinging the sickle.

Crowe turned and felt something strike him on his head. Instinctively, Crowe swung his old war Colt, hitting Burke across the neck, turning the killer on his heel. But before he could level his pistol, the sickle blade came down again. Boone's pistol tumbled to the dirt floor. Blood slid down the side of his face, but he pushed past the pain and lunged for Burke, whose excitement at seeing blood, shrieked out a laugh.

Boone tackled Burke and pressed his elbow into the killer's throat, but once more the sickle came down, the blunt handle hitting Crowe alongside his temple. Instantly the old marshal felt a wave of weakness pass over him. His hold slackened.

Cletus Burke pushed off Crowe and rose to his feet. Tossing the sickle aside, he drew his own pistol, but Iron Hand had heard the struggle. And she came through the barn door, pistol pointing in front of her. Seeing Boone on the ground, the scene froze her, just long enough for Burke to pull back the hammer and point his gun at the girl's face.

Suddenly, as if shot out of a cannon, the little black dog was in the air, and without warning hit Burke headlong, sinking her tiny, needle-sharp teeth into the killer's neck. Stunned, Burke howled in pain. His pistol fired wild, missing the girl. Trying to fight off the animal, Margot hung on in determined fury and forced the deserter backward where he fought for his footing but stumbled over his own fire and fell. Margot, tasting Burke's blood, grew savage.

Boone Crowe was up now, unsteady but able to retrieve his pistol, he stepped to the threshing man and kicked him alongside his head. The girl pulled her still-fighting dog away, and Boone Crowe, standing over Burke, put his boot on the deserter's gun hand. The girl pulled the revolver from Burke's hand, and just as Boone had done, she struck the deserter on the head with his own pistol, once, twice, until he slumped.

The fight was over. And the search was over.

Iron Hand went to Boone Crowe and looked at the blood. The first blow from the sickle blade had cut through Boone's scalp, knocking off his hat. The second cut was just above the left eyebrow. Both were still bleeding, but he waved away the girl's attentions.

"Later," he said.

She held Margot, who remained agitated. For a small, smooth-haired black dog with a sweet and friendly face, her protective nature had saved the girl's life. She held the animal tight until the dog's spirited heart calmed.

But Boone Crowe was staring at the fugitive with a hatred like a choke hold around his own heart. Lancelot Tunneson was a friend who'd shared battles with him, down south in Apache and Comanche country. They had talked of dreams and of loves together. And at long last, Lancelot had found that love in the pretty Turtle Woman.

Burke shook himself awake. Crowe bent down and grabbed the killer by the shirt. Then he yanked Burke to his feet. Blood dripped from Boone's cheek and chin onto his shirt collar. He barely realized that he was still holding his pistol.

"Are you Cletus Burke, a deserter from Fort Laramie?"

Burke shook his head, one hand at his torn and bleeding neck. "Ye be mistaken."

Iron Hand approached and pointed to the mutilated ear. Then she spit in his face. "You lie."

"So what if I am, you Indian bitch?" he answered.

She put the dog back on the ground, and then rearing back, she punched him hard in the face with her small fist. More blood gushed, this time from Burke's nose. She reached down and picked up the growling Margot.

Burke smiled a madman's macabre grin, his face a red mess.

"You are the last of them," Boone said.

A look of bewilderment replaced the twisted smile.

"The others are all dead, Burke. Murphy and Byrnes. O'Clery and Quinn."

"And Baby Sullivan," the girl added.

It was an oddly quiet moment that followed. Finally Boone

spoke to the girl. "It's time to go. See if you can gather up the horses."

Iron Hand looked at him, seeing something strange in the old marshal's eyes. She studied him for a moment longer, but didn't argue. Calling for Margot to follow, she left the barn, glancing one last time over her shoulder, and then she searched for the extra horses that grazed in the wet grass. She was nearly to them when she heard the gunshot. Her heart did not jump. She had been expecting it. In fact, she had welcomed it. Cletus Burke would now belong to the barn rats. She knew that Boone Crowe would leave him there, his black heart on the underside of Hell.

Chapter 20

THE STORM MOVED EAST into the Dakota country, and Bright Cohen and Henry Mussel watched like a pair of old pioneers as the clouds swept into new open country. They found shelter in an outcropping of rocks where a series of runner ravines coursed the landscape. Both of them sat wordless during the worst of the snowfall, each with his mind on the future, of where to go and what to do. Since Cohen was essentially a dead man, he needed to shed himself of his army uniform and change his name.

The ex-private had been on patrols with Sergeant Tunneson and knew something of the country. Having made a loop of their travels, he figured they were less than fifty miles from Ft. Tillman. There was the rail station there and stores. But also a gaggle of army troops on leave or assignment there too. If he could walk unnoticed into to the mercantile as a soldier and walk out as a civilian, he might be able to make his first step to freedom.

Ft. Tillman was a wide-open town too, of every kind of humanity, from cow punchers, freighters, businessmen, whores, and church-goers. Indians too were not a scarce commodity either, so long as they stayed out of everyone's way. Most of the citizens of Ft. Tillman had enough on their minds and wouldn't add Indian trouble to their lists. So Henry Mussel would likely blend in, for the time being anyway.

"If I can scrape up enough money for a train ticket," he said, "I reckon I'll just head back to Indiana. The old farm ain't exactly paradise, but it's sounding better all the time."

Henry shrugged in stoic Indian fashion. "I know only horses. Mr. Peacock. He pay me for that. I fix mean horses. Make tame."

"Well, the right place will have a job for you. I'm sure of that." Cohen knew that the young Indian was still nursing a hurt heart over the dead girl. And who could blame him? Henry had spoken of her with words Cohen had never heard come from an Indian before. Cohen had never had a girl but didn't plan on that being his life story. There'd been plenty of them on his mind since joining the army, mostly farm gals from his early days. Some of them might still be around. If not, there'd sure be new ones. Most of the girls he knew also had younger sisters.

First things first, he thought.

Henry Mussel was in mourning. There was no way to hide it. It would be difficult to find another girl whose face was like the spring flowers. And her voice like the rippling of the water.

With these thoughts, the two mismatched friends rode quietly out of the storm and into the promise of a late sun toward Ft. Tillman.

A young runner scrambled down the boardwalk from the train station and turned his legs into pistons as he cut across side streets and empty lots until he reached the door of the woman, Yelena, whom he knew had just had a baby. Springfield, Illinois, after all, was not so big that a messenger boy didn't know pretty much where and how everybody lived.

He knocked twice, as was his custom, and it was a lady with long, brown hair who answered.

"Message, ma'am. For Mrs. Crowe."

"Why, that's me." She fished in her apron for a coin, handed it to the boy, and then stood looking at the folded paper.

Rose. I am at the train station with my wife, hoping I might see you before we continue east. Signed, Rud Lacrosse.

"Oh no," she said out loud. Her first thought was for Boone. Had something happened to him? She went to the nursery and told Yelena about the note and that she was going immediately to the train station.

Rud and Paige stood when Rose of Sharon came through the station door. Seeing her worried face, he brushed her unspoken fears away. "Boone's fine. At least, that's not why I'm here."

Rose's shoulders sagged in relief.

For the next half hour Rud Lacrosse told her everything,

about his new job, about accepting it, and about having to leave without seeing Boone. "I heard he was on a mustang roundup, somewhere down by Fort Laramie. I imagine he was just having too much fun to stay in one place long enough to get my message."

The former marshal and Rose of Sharon stood in silence for a long moment.

Finally Paige Lacrosse cut in with a womanly question. "How is Yelena? And the baby?"

The tactic brought everyone out of their temporary stupor.

"Oh, the baby. The boy, Isaac, why...he's a healthy little lamb. And Yelena, resting well and doing well." She paused, then added, "I'll be leaving for Buffalo again. In another week, probably."

"I owe half my life to Boone," Rud said with unmasked passion. "He pulled me out of my fear back at Fort Tillman years ago. Starkweather put a noose around my neck and managed to hang my courage from a tree. But Boone, he pinned the badge back on me and showed that he trusted me. I'll always be obliged to him. For that and a thousand other things. I left a note with the one-armed preacher, but it didn't do much to express my true feelings. If you tell him, please, I would appreciate it."

Rose smiled and took the young man's hand. "He likely already knows it. But I'll tell him."

They parted with best wishes.

As Rose of Sharon walked back to Yelena's house, she thought, *A mustang roundup?*

"I wonder," she said, with a measure of doubt.

Boone Crowe left the barn, looking bloodied and worn down. By the old abandoned house he found a mossy tree stump and sat down. He removed his bandana, but before he could clean himself, Iron Hand was there with a canteen and poured water on it. Then, taking the bandana from him, she dabbed gingerly at the blood until she found its source and examined it.

"I feel a hundred years old," he said, mostly to himself.

The girl said nothing, only applied pressure to the wounds.

Still holding his old army Colt, he opened the cylinder and removed the spent cartridge. Then, reaching into his vest pocket, he removed four more spent casings and held all five in his palm. "Five bullets," he said, his voice trance-like. "I rode down to Fort Laramie to see my friend. Instead...I buried him. And then I killed five men." He put the five empty cartridges back in his vest pocket and looked up at the girl. "You're one hell of a beautiful girl. I could never have done it without you. How do I thank you?"

"You just did," she said.

The ground soaked up what was left of the snow and rain. The air wasn't warm but it wasn't bitter cold anymore either. They took account of the horses, one more counting Burke's, all of which belonged to the girl now through natural inheritance. At least, that's how Boone explained it to her. "I have a corral big enough to hold 'em," he said. "Until you decide what you plan to do."

Iron Hand gave no answer to this. She had other things on her mind. "What if someone reports us to the law?"

"Let 'em."

"A lot of people saw us do the killing."

He looked at her as they climbed into their saddles. "We'll take it as it comes."

Together they rode until dusk. Then they made a camp in the lee of a ridge where the wind could not bother them. While they had ridden, they passed the place where they'd huddled together under the fallen tree, and Boone Crowe remembered how he'd squeezed in beside the girl and put his arm around her, in an effort to keep her warm. He had felt his heart pounding against her heart, and he remembered the way it felt to love. In about three days he would be back home at his little ranch in the valley outside of Buffalo.

Around the campfire, watching the blackened coffee pot

bubble, he wondered much. How was Rufus doing, taking care of everything all alone at the ranch, what with Rose and him both being gone so long? How much would he tell Rose? About all this? Would he tell her anything? And there was a vision again. Pup Murphy, lying naked on the whore's bed. Hands held up. *What? Wait?* Is that what he'd said? Boone couldn't remember. He just remembered killing the kid. In a cold-blooded rage.

Iron Hand was pampering Margot. The dog had proven heroic; they both knew it. If Buckboard Bob hadn't agreed to part with the little pooch, who could tell what might have happened. Burke might have killed the girl. Boone could justify his killing Burke, to some degree, but if something had happened to Isabel, it would have destroyed him. He had mishandled the whole affair in the barn.

"You look like the cat who ate the bird, Boone."

He nodded. "It shows, huh?"

"I probably look the same."

Crowe knelt at the fire and poured coffee into his tin cup. "Want some?"

"Not now."

"Whisky would be better." He tried to sound light, but it didn't work. "We don't have any, though."

"Just as well. You know what whisky does to Indians."

"I've heard."

"And I've seen."

Boone sipped carefully at the hot brew. "I've been thinking," he said.

"I would never have guessed."

This made him smile, and it felt strange, as if his face might come apart in pieces. "Well, for starters, what you planning on doing with that scalp?"

"Why?"

"Well, I reckon you was within yer rights to do it. But...it kind of stole some things from you."

She studied him. "Things like what?'

He drank more from his cup, stalling, knowing he'd just stepped into a trap. A trap he'd laid himself.

The girl waited, staring at him.

"Things that an old fool sees. Nothing more."

"After what we just come through, I would think most of our secrets were out."

Boone took off his hat and bristled up his hair. Then, back went the hat. "I ain't talkin secrets. Not really. Jist how I see things, and they're probably old fashioned."

Her dark eyes bore into him.

"Do you realize, Isabel, that you speak better English than I do?"

It was her turn to smile. "Survival, Boone Crowe. Practice and survival. It was a weapon."

"Well, words come outta yer mouth in a mighty pretty way."

"You are trying hard to change the subject. What are your 'some things'?"

He could hear the click of the trap, and now he had nowhere to go but to put his foot in his mouth and be done with it. "I have a friend. Name a' Tugs Bigelow. He and I have had our disagreements in the past. He's a horse trader from Sheridan country. Red whiskers and a turned-up scout's hat."

Iron Hand sat patiently.

"Anyway, old Tugs, who ain't really old...but anyway, he likes to make a joke out of my simple ways. But what I tell this bachelor is, at least I know love when I see it. And then he takes up callin me a romantic. He means that as a joke too, but, well, I think otherwise. I take it as a compliment."

"Is there a meaning to this story?"

"There is. It's jist a bit hard to spit out. Seein as how you are the subject of my mutterings. Besides, I think yer jist trying to talk me past my misery."

She shook her head. "I think there will be plenty left over. For both of us."

"Okay, then. Here it is. Even though I understand you doin

it, it pained me to have you kill that Byrnes fella. And then the scalpin of Baby Sullivan. I know that sort of thing goes back a long ways. It's jist...dammit girl, you're makin me sweat."

She waited.

"Call it what you want. But it takes away from how I want to see you. Yer innocence. Yer beauty."

"I'm not innocent. I've been through too much."

"I know that, Isabel. I told you, I'm jist an old fool."

"And that's your secret? That you think I'm beautiful?"

"No. It's more than that. And it'll make you think I've lost the little sense I ever had in the first place."

"Well, Mr. Boone Crowe, neither of us are going anywhere tonight."

The old romantic drew in a breath. "I told you about Little Feet. And how, well, how I loved her. Wonderin, as I did then, and still do, was if she was, you know, carrying...my child. And knowin I'll never know, it has grieved me plenty over the years that...that I had no children of my own. A man wants when he's old what he never got when he was young."

The girl looked into the fire, trying to put Boone's words into a proper order.

"It wasn't my plan to speak of this. It was meant fer my own thinkin only. But I put my boot in it, so here it is, all spilled out."

"Tell it straight."

"I jist did."

"'Tell it straight,'" she said again.

"All right. Rather than havin you go around the country shootin and scalpin outlaws, I'd like to fetch you home with me. Rose of Sharon is childless too. And my ranch house, well, I was planning all along to add on a couple of rooms."

"For who?"

"Confound it, girl. You're like to twist me in a knot. For you, Isabel. For you, girl. Come with me home. And don't make me say it all again, cause I'm plumb talked out." He threw off his coffee dredges and stood.

"Where you think you're going?"

"Some place out there in the night where I can give myself a swift kick."

"Why?"

"You and yer questions."

The girl stood too. She started to speak but realized she had no words to say. It didn't matter anyway; the old marshal was already gone, stomping through the tall grass, disappearing into the face of the silver moon. She would tell him later about the scalp. She would tell him that she had left it lying in the tall grass of the trail many miles back, happy to be rid of it.

Fort Tillman was lit up, having only recently graduated into kerosene street lights. There weren't enough yet to brag about, but there were two on each side of the main street, which kept old Buzz Faulkner busy with the lighting and the extinguishing every day. Otherwise he was the chief cabinet maker in town and filling in with the coffin making whenever a customer wanted something what Buzz called Back-East-Fancy. In Arkansas, where he'd sprung from, he had built a casket for a deceased former Confederate colonel. When he presented it to the dead colonel's family for inspection, they found a small trap door in the side. *What's this for?* they asked. *Why, that there's an escape hatch. In the chance some of his old Yank enemies come looking to dig him up.*

Buzz Faulkner was the first person Bright Cohen and Henry Mussel saw when they rode into town. Buzz stood on his short ladder, putting a torch to the last of his lamps. The two horsemen reined in and watched him work.

"Ain't much, I know, fellas," Buzz said over his shoulder. "Cheyenne, it's told, got itself electric streetlights. We ain't there yet, but it's a comin."

"Electric, you say," commented Cohen.

"Plumb magic to me," Buzz said, descending his ladder. "Or

black magic. I seen plenty a that too, where I come from."

"Well," Cohen went on, "beings as how it's approachin dark, I suppose the mercantile is closed up."

"Ha, mister. This here's Fort Tillman. Nothin closes here. We got three mercantile stores, and you're practically standin atop the best of the three." He pointed to an illuminated window half a block away.

"Much obliged," Cohen said, and Buzz Faulkner tipped his hat in reply.

They tied their horses to the rail in front of the store and mounted the boardwalk. "I need outta these army clothes. I got about two dollars to my name. Wish me luck, Henry."

Until he could be shed of his uniform, the two men had agreed to play it safe. No need to draw unwanted attention to themselves. Henry Mussel waited outside in the shadows with the horses while Cohen went inside to strike a bargain. After a casual look around, the clerk, who was watching him, spoke up.

"We do a little laundering in the back. That uniform looks like it could use some attention. No offense meant, of course."

Cohen smiled. "Truth be told, sir, I'm fixin to be rid of it. I just fulfilled my enlistment, and I'm a free man. I was hopin to strike up a trade."

The clerk came around the counter and examined the uniform. Aside from the prairie dirt and sweat, he nodded approvingly. "We do a little army business here. Wash these up, and I might be able to do a trade. Nothing fancy, though, mind you. Look around and find something you can settle on. There's a changing room behind that curtain."

In ten minutes the trade was done.

"I could use a spare shirt. What will a dollar buy me?"

The clerk pointed to a shelf stacked with used shirts and trousers. "There's some nice linen shirts in there yet. The best have been picked over. I don't recommend the linsey-woolsey. A little stiff at the collar."

"I fear I am at your mercy with my questions. My partner and

I need a place to spread our blankets, but you done got my last dollar."

The storekeeper rubbed his chin. "For how long?"

"Till I can make enough money for a train ride back to Indiana."

"Well, there's jobs to be had here, but they ain't pretty ones. But, as for sleeping cheap, I'd send you up the street. Way up the street, up past Whore Town. It's where the one-armed preacher holds court. He's been known to help a lost soul when they show up."

"Up the street, you say?"

"Yep. Them gals will be hooting at you when you pass through. You can just pay them no mind. The preacher's tent has a flag hanging from it. Got a big red cross on it. Can't miss it. Even in the dark."

"Well, sir, that's mighty helpful. At this moment, lost souls is exactly what we are."

Outside, Cohen gave the spare shirt to Henry, and together they headed up the wide, dusty lane, the street lamps fading behind them into four twinkles in the night.

Chapter 21

THE TWO RIDERS TURNED north. Sometimes the dog rode in the saddle with the girl; sometimes it ran ahead, sniffing out a rabbit scent, always keeping the little caravan in sight. Even with a bright sun, the air felt cold. Boone Crowe knew the weather patterns of Wyoming Territory and the way winter could come down like a hammer stroke. The air gave a hint of that several days ago and he knew more would be coming soon.

After two long days of riding, they entered into the heavily treed hills surrounding Buffalo. Boone purposely wanted to avoid the town for the time being, deciding rather to skirt it and head straight for the ranch. Even though Rose wouldn't be there yet, his anxiety grew. The awkward subject of Iron Hand staying with them had not come up again, and he felt it best to let it rest. But he was sure she was thinking about it, or thinking about something because he could count the words she had spoken these past two days on the fingers of one hand.

At last, crossing over the final hill, there below them was the ranch, chimney smoke rising from Rufus's half of the dog-run. The sun was at its zenith, and the fenced pasture against the far hillside held a mix of cows grazing. The corral was empty, but even from here Boone could see Rufus puttering in the yard. When he looked up and recognized Boone, Rufus waved and then danced a silly jig. He opened the gate to the corral. Rufus forked a couple of lumps of hay in the pen and waited as Boone herded the string of horses inside. Once corralled, Rufus closed the gate. After taking a brief glance at the girl, Rufus hollered a *howdy-do.*

"Boy o' boy, Boone, you been on an adventure, I can see that. And who's this pretty little tulip, if I might ask?"

"Rufus," Boone said, "this here is..."

"Boone calls me Isabel," the girl said, cutting him off.

Boone gave her a sideways look. "She..." He closed his mouth and smiled.

Rufus started in his toothless jabber, "Sure am glad to see you, marshal. Plenty tired of people ridin out here askin about you. Judge Schaffer rode out three...no, four times. Once already this morning. He says, where's Crowe? Where's Crowe, goin on like an old croaky rooster? And I tell him, I reckon we'll all know when he gits back."

"Who else?"

"That deputy of yours. That lovesick Wales kid."

"He's not my deputy. He works for Rud."

"Well, old Rud was out oncet too. Near a week on, I'd say."

"Anyone else?"

"That boy who runs errands for the judge. Toby what's-his-name. Come out on that mule a his. Left a telygram fer ya. It's in the house. I left it on the table in there."

"What's it say?"

Rufus gave Boone a curious look. "You know I ain't the readin kind. I mean, Mrs. Crowe taught me my letters, but I ain't no snoop. It's yer telygram anyway, not mine."

The girl had wandered off, making a show of following Margot, who was snooping out the place, but Boone saw it as something else. "I'll have a look at that telegram," he said. He was going to ask the girl to come in the house, but she had drifted farther into the field behind the house, and so he let her be.

Boone read the message: *Must stay another week.* It was dated two days earlier. *I will keep in touch. All's well. Rose.*

If all's well, then it must be something else, he reasoned, and he knew what it was. Yelena had been part of her family for so long that parting was difficult. She had even hinted something to that effect before she left. *Mercy me,* she'd said. *To see that dear girl again will be heavenly. And a baby.* She had lady friends in Buffalo, but it wasn't quite the same. He remembered his foolish talk with Iron Hand. Looking out the kitchen window he saw that she was sitting on an old fence rail out in the tall grass, her pretty head showing the signs of deep concentration.

Boone moved around inside the house, breathing in the

familiar air. Rufus had kept his own room across the dog-run heated, but the house was chilly, so he fired up the potbelly stove in the kitchen and made the fixings for a fire in the hearth. After wasting another handful of minutes, he went out to the field where the girl continued to sit and ponder. He sat on the rail beside her but did not readily speak.

After a while, Iron Hand, looking down at the ground in front of her, said, "They cut our hair. Boys and girls, both. Our hair is part of our spiritual connection to the world. I think they knew that. That is why they did it."

Boone listened, knowing she was talking about the white man's Indian school in Omaha.

"They punished us if we spoke Lakota. English only." She lifted her gaze to the pined hillsides surrounding the ranch and breathed-in the fresh scent. "I have not forgotten. Not any of it. All the way back to Willow Creek. All the way back to the killing in the village. The gathering of us children afterward. The train ride. The beatings. The humiliation. Running away did not work. They found me. Twice. And brought me back."

It was hard for Boone to hear this, though none of it was new to his ears. He wanted desperately to comfort her, but knew she was going someplace with these remembrances, and he wanted to give her the time she needed.

"Uncle Pea sent for me. But it took years. By then I had learned the white man's tongue. It was my weapon. I learned it so well I was made a teacher for the little ones that came after. They always came. Frightened faces."

Boone Crowe imagined she still saw those faces.

"But...a long time ago, back then. Back in Willow Creek, I learned that not all white people are bad. It was the day I saw you." She took hold of one of her long black braids and caressed the end of it, as if a comforting talisman. "And then you came for me again. As if out of a dream. And I learned how big Boone Crowe's heart is." She turned and faced him finally. "I may never find a heart that big again."

It was Boone's turn to look into the girl's face, the remaining swipes of war paint across both cheeks, the two raven feathers she had stuck in her hair, the pretty lips and the dark eyes.

She reached out with her fair hand and took the rough hand of the old marshal. She held it for a long time. "I have no place to go...where I will be better loved."

They sat on the rail for a while until finally Boone put his arm around the girl's shoulder. He felt her shudder slightly and then move close.

Bright Cohen had already found work digging a drainage ditch behind the bank to let off waste water from the recent rain. It was not appealing work, but it paid, and soon he knew that pipes would be laid. There were parts of Fort Tillman that were advancing, so he felt fortunate to get any kind of work. Every day was a train ride closer to Indiana. But there was a thorn in this thinking too, as he was starting to get accustomed to civilian life again, and though the town was a bit rough around the edges, the one-armed preacher had shown great generosity by giving he and Henry a place to sleep at night. The reverend did, of course, expect to see both of them in the church tent on Sunday.

Henry Mussel, in his white man's clothes was not harassed, in spite of his braids and dark skin. Fort Tillman was indeed a place so deeply blended that making a fuss about a man's origins was a case of the pot calling the kettle black. Henry had seen much worse in his time and wished there were more places like this in the country. On Sunday he found himself sitting in the one-armed preacher's church tent, squeezed between a prostitute and a hungover cowpoke, with no mention of pride at all. It didn't take long before his knowledge of horses found him employed a few hours a day at the livery stable, feeding and sweeping out stalls. Like Cohen, he would take what he could.

But Henry Mussel maintained a stoic silence, his mind

often wandering back to the trading post and his two friends, Bull Head and Iron Hand, now both dead. He remembered Mr. Peacock finding him on the reservation, breaking the few mustangs Indians were allowed to catch and keep. Bull Head was already working for him, so the days were passed in doing what he loved, working with horse flesh. He had erected his own tipi next to Bull Head's, and together they helped Mr. Peacock make a business of horse trading.

Then one day, the girl arrived from the east, and Henry Mussel became immediately taken by her beauty. But she was bitter and so he was careful at first, giving her a wide berth as if she were the ruling goose in the barnyard. She used to come to the fence and watch him breaking the latest wild horses Mr. Peacock brought in. One day Henry was thrown to the ground by a stubborn roan, and after standing up and dusting himself off, he saw the girl laughing. It was the opening for a week of wordless exchanges of the eyes, which eventually turned into shy words. The girl, Iron Hand, was wary and picked her words carefully. She spoke mostly English, a language taught to him by Mrs. Peacock in the year before the girl arrived. It was different to be forced to learn English by a white teacher, and something else to be taught English by an Indian woman who learned it from someone who loved her.

In the stable, though, on this day, these memories were too bitter to dwell on, so he turned his sad murmurings to the horses. They had seen their own sad days, as most creatures had.

In the darkness of his bedroom, in his own bed at last, Boone Crowe woke with a start. They had been standing there, beneath the window where the moon's gray glow had thrown a ghostly light. Cletus Burke, O'Clery, Quinn, Baby Sullivan, and Pup Murphy. The five of them, standing shoulder to shoulder, as if on roll call. Each wore his fatal bloody wounds, and his eyes, giving off his own condemning light, stared unblinking and terrifying.

Sweating, Boone sat up in his bed. This was not like the frequent nightmares about Cold Harbor and the battle of the Wilderness. This was new and convicting. He nearly tipped over the lamp trying to light it, and once lit, he sat trembling. He wondered if he had cried out, hoping he had not, as Iron Hand slept in the next room. Sitting, waiting for a sound from her, he felt relief when none came.

He dressed and crept into the kitchen. The dog's paws padded on the floor behind him, but a gentle pat on the head sent the animal back to the girl's room. Boone stared out the kitchen window into the night. *They're out there,* he thought. *Waiting for my confession.*

When Iron Hand woke in the morning and dressed, she saw Boone in the yard talking to a man with a top hat and long coat standing beside a surrey pulled by a black horse. The man was smaller than Boone, but there appeared an air of authority around him. Boone was shaking his head, and the other man turned his back and took a couple of steps away with his gloved hands clenched behind him. Finally he returned to Boone. Now it seemed the authority had moved from the stranger to Boone, and whatever they were talking about, Boone seemed to be in charge.

Iron Hand watched with curiosity as the man climbed into his surrey and with a flick of the reins took the trail over the hill as Boone watched him go. Even after the wagon was long gone, he remained there, as if seeing into a dim future.

"I've got some business to attend to," he said, after returning to the house. They sat at the kitchen table. "Rose's train will be coming in to Fort Tillman in three days. I need those days to settle some things."

"Am I coming with you?"

"Not this time. You'll be perfectly safe here. You have two watch dogs—Margot and Rufus. And, the room you slept in, that's yours now. Until I add a couple more on the back. Might not be till spring. So make it your own."

"Where are you going?"

"I owe someone a debt. And then I need to see a friend in Fort Tillman. Before Rose comes in."

The girl frowned. "I'm afraid," she said. "Afraid she won't like me."

"You talk to Rufus about that. If I can't rest your mind, he'll sure be able to."

He watched as her shoulders sank and then rose.

"Who was that man?"

"Judge Schaffer. He jist gave me a bit of news."

"It must be bad news. You don't look happy."

"Happy for the man, Rud Lacrosse. Sad for Wyoming Territory." He told her what he knew, about Rud resigning and heading back east. He didn't tell her the rest, though.

"When are you leaving?"

"I shoulda left already. But I wanted to tell you."

"Are you okay?"

"I'm dandy, girl."

"You are a very poor liar, Boone Crowe."

This time he rode straight, no sidetracks to inspect bodies or bury bodies; the vultures and wolves would have them by now anyway. And that would be for another person, one more presently humane than an ex-marshal gone bad. Boone's mind swung back and forth like this as he and the Ghost Horse retraced much of the same country he and Iron Hand had just traveled. But if his mind would ever be settled, he had to do this.

He decided to rest his horse often, but he would continue on through the night because there would be other business after this. Rose's train was something he couldn't miss. There was the weather too. Wyoming winters were a cross between sneak thieves and ambush raiders, coming without the curtesy of warning. And when they fell, they fell hard. If he could get all this out of the way before a storm hit, all the better. So under moonlight he rode, stopping once in the early morning to kindle a coffee fire and rub down the Ghost Horse. From there his destination was only a few more hours.

And dawn found him there, staring at the undisturbed ruins of the old trading post, the corrals, and the remaining tipi. But something was different. Someone had buried the dead horses. Burned and buried. And there were the iron shod tracks of an army mount, coming in and leaving. And the tracks were deeper on their leaving. The rider, whoever it was, left with a burden. Boone might follow them for a while after he was finished here.

Dismounting, Boone Crowe walked solemnly up the slope to the stand of trees and the big grave that he had dug and then buried what remained of his friend Tunneson and the others. And here too where footprints. Boots and moccasins. Finally, he reached inside his coat and retrieved the five spent .45 cartridges from his pocket and held them in his gloved hand. Then, with his other hand, he scooped out a small cup of dirt from the grave top and dropped in the five casings. Then he smoothed back the dirt and stood.

"Lancelot, my friend. You and your fellow sufferers have been avenged. It has cost me my honor, but it is done. My regrets are my own to bear."

Chapter 22

IT WAS QUITTING TIME, another day's work finished and shovel man Bright Cohen climbed out of his trench, muddy clay covering the front of his pants and shirt. He had just enough money from his first two days' work to buy a second outfit. He'd put his dirty clothes in a washtub and let them hang on the line outside the tent. With cold nights they'd be clean but iron stiff. He hoped the old storekeeper would let him in the place, dirty as he was. As he walked, he saw a rider appear out of the sun's sinking red glow. He was chewing on a slab of jerky, but upon seeing the rider, Cohen's jaws went slack. *I know that man,* he thought. *That's Boone Crowe.*

Cohen made a feeble attempt at sprucing himself but gave up. He stood in the street and waited. As the rider drew near, Cohen called out, "Mister Crowe, sir!"

Boone stopped his horse and looked at the young man, his expression twisted in vague recognition.

"Private Bright Cohen, Mr. Crowe. I'm the soldier that give you the names of the deserters. Remember?"

Boone stared, stunned. "Why, yes...I do remember. But..."

"It's a long story, sir. One you might want to hear. And...I reckon I got questions for you too. If you've a mind."

Five minutes later, in the closest saloon, Cohen spoke about his faked death and desertion, all for the sake of finding his sergeant. Crowe followed along with his own story and the grisly details of what he found.

"Are you the one that buried 'em?"

Boone nodded soberly. "What's this about an Indian?" he asked.

"Henry Mussel. He was there when I got to the burned-out trading post. He had been bad wounded. Claims old Straw Dog tended to him."

"Alive, you say." This was interesting news.

"Oh sure. He's alive in body. His spirits are down a heap,

though. Frettin over the Indian girl gettin killed and all."

"Iron Hand?"

"Yes sir. That's the one. Tore up Henry real bad."

Crowe smiled under his drooping mustache. "Is he here?"

"Yup. We got here a couple days back. He's doin some work at the livery."

"Well, he'll wanna hear the news I bring. The girl lives."

Cohen's eyes became round saucers.

"And the girl thinks Henry Mussel is dead."

Bright Cohen shook his head. "If that don't beat all. Hell's a fire. Henry might plumb fly circles around this town, hearin this news."

"Listen," Boone said, "the girl's at my little spread up at Buffalo. She's helpin mind the place. My wife's comin in on the morning train. He can ride back with me."

"Henry'd crawl back if he had to."

"All right, Cohen. This is a heap of story. We both have more to tell. But I have business with the one-armed preacher."

"That's where we're stayin."

"My business is private. But why don't you tell Henry that I want to see him later? Go ahead and give him the news, but the details will have to wait till later."

"Yessir."

"You fixin to stay here? You need anything. Money?"

"I got a little. Enough to buy another pair of clothes. Maybe."

"You like yer job?"

"Look at me, sir. Bein mistaken for a hog in a waller ain't much of a job."

"Well, you go buy yer new duds. We'll talk later. I'll be at the Pathfinder Hotel. Around eight."

Cohen stood, shook hands, and left.

Boone Crowe considered having a whisky but thought better of it. Even the beer setting before him had lost its luster.

The potbellied stove inside the one-armed preacher's tent was throwing out a comfortable heat. Removing his customary black flop hat, the preacher folded his hands in his lap and waited, his old friend sitting like a stone statue on a bench. Finally he asked, "What troubles you, marshal?"

"A good many things." He shook his head. "No...a *bad* many things."

The fire popped and Boone Crowe flinched.

Outside the tent a whore's screech filled the night.

"Murder," Crowe whispered.

The preacher waited.

It was as if the heat from the stove had a sound, a murmuring. Boone swallowed and in the dim light of the tent told all, from the discovery of the bodies at the trading post and the trading post itself, reduced to cinders. He spoke of his rage and his heartbreak. Finally he told about the killing of each of the men. How he murdered Pup Murphy in cold blood. O'Clery and Quinn he gave a chance to fight, a poor chance. Baby Sullivan was a crazed dog who had killed Amadeus Peacock and his wife and Bull Head. He left nothing out; except he did not speak of the girl having killed the stupid follower, Byrnes. He only spoke of her as his companion, having seen their faces. And then there was Cletus Burke, the man who brutally killed his friend, Sergeant Lancelot Tunneson, in a most horrible way. He spoke of how, in the barn, he told Burke of his sins before killing him.

"I am no better than the men I have hunted," he said, these last words spoken so quietly the one-armed preacher thought his friend might be close to weeping.

"The good book is filled with similar deeds, Boone. King David is only one. But I ask you, is this your confession?"

Boone sighed. "I just needed to talk. So I guess you've heard it."

"Then I have it in my power to absolve you of your sins."

The old marshal made no sound.

"There was a woman caught in adultery once, in Bible times. She was about to be stoned by her accusers, but the Lord intervened. He challenged those who persecuted her. 'Who is sinless among you', He said. When they departed, the Lord spoke to the woman and said, 'Neither do I condemn you. Go and sin no more.'"

Boone lifted his head, his eyes reflecting the firelight.

"I can only tell you the same. I do absolve you, my friend. But I wish never to have these kinds of confessions again."

Crowe's shoulders lifted. "I won't. I mean I can't. The burden's too heavy. And...I fear what Rose of Sharon will think."

"I think Rose would understand more than you realize. She knows she did not marry a choir boy. But I believe she knows who you are inside. A lesser man wouldn't be here with me right now."

Boone Crowe stood. "Rud resigned," he said suddenly.

"I know. He left this note for you." He lifted the folded paper from his small desk and handed it to Boone. He looked at it then handed it back to the preacher. "Will you read it, please? My courage might fail me."

Boone, I tried to find you before leaving. Would have liked to see you one last time. I owe you more than I can say in a simple note like this. Forgive me for leaving you in the lurch. Life has taken a turn. A good one, I think. My greatest respect for you, Boone, for pulling me out of the ditch of doubt and helping me stand up again. Your loyal deputy, Rud Lacrosse.

Boone touched his whiskers. "He was a fine deputy. Judge Schaffer wants me to take my old job back."

"I know."

"How? How'd you know?"

The one-armed preacher winked. "Don't ask me to reveal all my secrets."

At the tent flap Boone turned. "Should I take the job? I mean, considering..." He waved his hand as if referring to the words that the night had held. "Considering all this."

"The way to the rest of our lives is forward, my friend. Not backward. Go in peace."

The night was moonless and black. Captain Stephen Gillespie sat at his desk sorting through some papers. Before him was the report he had been preparing for Colonel Beach, who would be returning within the week from back east. In his mind, Gillespie harbored a hope that the train Beach was on would derail and the damn colonel would be killed. That would likely secure him a promotion to major and the official command of Fort Laramie until its closure. From there, who knew?

What he wrestled with, in his report, was how to explain the disappearance of Sergeant Tunneson. The man had never returned from his pursuit of the six deserters, which was another black mark on the report. Desertion was nothing new. It had even occurred when Beach was here, commanding every day. He would gladly list them as killed in action with the hostiles, along with Private Cohen, rather than as deserters. But if he did that, he'd have to list Tunneson as the one who deserted. But that damn Private Martin Cochran would see that for what it was: a lie.

He put down the papers. *Enough for tonight,* he thought. *I still have a day or two to figure this out.* He buttoned his uniform blouse, put on his hat, and blew out the candle. Walking across the parade ground to his billets, a deeper, more sinister thought presented itself. *What if Colonel Beach had an accident here? Let him get settled in.* He wasn't a particular favorite with the men. They might see it as a favor.

These were the thoughts he carried with him as he ambled through the darkness. Then he stopped, almost giddy with the sudden forming of the perfect plan. He stood, putting the pieces together, when he heard the softest of steps behind him. Turning, he saw the dull form of a man, but he made not a sound as the hatchet blade was buried into his head, splitting his skull like a pumpkin. By the time the sun came up and the first of the soldiers filed out of their tents and found Gillespie lying there dead, Straw Dog was many miles away.

Chapter 23

It was late November and winter showed its teeth. The two riders stopped on the top of the hill and stared down at the twin trails of smoke rising in the gray afternoon sky, one from the house chimney and the other from the smoke hole of the tipi, erected on the far side of the pasture where the little creek, already frosted over, shown silver in the late sun.

Marshal Boone Crowe and his deputy Bright Cohen had just delivered their prisoner into Judge Schaffer's custody and were now ready to report to the two chief Thanksgiving cooks down yonder, Rose of Sharon and Isabel. There was a marvel to the past events, as if they had been laid out years, maybe even centuries, ago. Boone was starting to believe such things. The tragedy of the Peacock Massacre, as it was being referred to in certain circles, with all of its heartache and death, had through mercies untold, spawned new life and love into a small group of survivors.

Rose had taken the news of the girl being part of a much-needed family like the true champion she was: with open arms. Even the tipi, the last thing remaining at the burnt trading post and transported by Henry Mussel in Indian fashion to the hillside away from the house, was seen by Rose as the way life should be, *a gathering,* as she called it. The two young people's courtship, which blossomed after their surprised and joyful reunion, moved at its own pace. And before the project had to be given up with the first heavy snow, Rufus and Henry had managed to lay the rock foundation for another small house on a back acre.

At Rose's bidding, a new table, much bigger and of local birch, had been built for this very occasion. More candles were arranged and with chairs circling the table, and the supper bell was rung. The one-armed preacher gave the blessing, and soon the venison, wild turkey, sweet potatoes, and corn were put before them.

It was later, after Rufus had retired and Bright Cohen had ridden back into Buffalo with the one-armed preacher, when Boone Crowe made his customary visit to the corrals in the darkness. On this night he was joined by the girl, who saw him leave the house and followed him out. Together they stood at the fence rails and stared up at the moon, the only sound that of their frosty breathing in the chilly air. Finally Boone put his arm around the girl's shoulder and drew her close.

"I wish I had the proper words, Isabel."

"We don't need words, Mister Boone Crowe. Not anymore."

Then the old marshal did what he'd wanted to do for a long time. He kissed the girl on the forehead and told her he loved her.

ACKNOWLEDGEMENTS

As with all of my novels, there was a talented lineup of supporting help with *5 Bullets*, which begins with my faithful editor, Jennifer Moorman. She is the custodian who sweeps up and patches up the careless grammatical errors that fall from my pages after the first draft. Jennifer's loyalty to putting forth the best copy is priceless, and these few words of thanks fall far short of the praise she deserves. She has been my editor throughout this blessed writing journey.

Talent runs in the Moorman family, as sister, Alexandria, steps into the important role again as juggler of images and design for the book's cover, giving the proper touches that make a final product shine with reader appeal. She is a valuable member of the team.

In *5 Bullets*, the cover photographs are the fine work of Rachel Thornton Boruff, talented photographer and owner and operator of Rozzie Rayne Studio Props. Her work has appeared on many of my book covers.

My most sincere appreciation for my cover model, Cheyenne Andrews, whose dedication to this project was exceptional and long running, and for our many years of delightful friendship. Half Colville Indian herself, she provided the perfect blend of beauty and attitude to the shoot. Cheyenne's costar on this book, Stella the dog, made the session that much more fun. I thank Stella's owner, my son Alex J. E. Buchmann, for loaning her out, which proved a treat for everyone.

Finally, but in no way lastly, thank you to my wife, Rebecca, who provides me with all kinds of missing ingredients, from both gentle to brutal opinion, to proofreading final texts with her yellow highlighter, which she welds like a lightsaber. She has been my right hand of support from the very beginning, thirteen books ago, and I could never have done it without her.

I have heard some authors say that writing is "just a lot of hard work," as if that was the sum and total of their efforts. More's the pity, as I've never seen it that way. After each book I finish, I often stand in amazement for a talent given to me by God that both mystifies and gratifies me. The stories that fill my pages come from a deep well, previously undisturbed, until the time is right to draw them up, one bucket at a time. And to this mystery of imagination, I am just the water-bearer.

About the Author

E. Hank Buchmann, who also writes westerns under the pseudonym, Buck Edwards, lives in the uncluttered prairies of eastern Washington State, with his wife, Rebecca, where the velvety red sunsets are without compare. Raised on a cattle and wheat ranch, Buchmann's love for the open spaces has given him an appreciation for the hardworking pioneers—men and women—who shaped its history.

A lifelong lover of books, Buchmann grew up under the pages of Zane Grey; Conrad Richter; Willa Cather, and later Cormac McCarthy; Jim Harrison; and Robert Olmsted, as well as the exceptional book *Ben Snipes: Northwest Cattle King* by Roscoe Sheller. Living and working within range of the Whitman Mission in Walla Walla; the old horse grazing and watering grounds of Chief Moses at Moses Lake; and the final track down of the outlaw Harry Tracy, inspiration is always close at hand.

The Boone Crowe western series, written under the pseudonym Buck Edwards, are *Dead Woman Creek*; *Showdown in the Bear Grass*; *Judgment at Rattlesnake Wash*; *Track of the Wolf*; *The Widow Makers*; *Shootout at Lost River*; and *5 Bullets*.

Buchmann's other novels are *Until the Names Grow Blurred*; *Darling Liberty*; *The Homing*; *Nightly Crossings*; and *Lila B.*, as well as a collection of poetry, *Natives of Lost Places*. Buchmann's books are available online through Amazon and Barnes and Noble, as well as select bookstores.

Follow along with E. Hank Buchmann on Facebook.

Made in the USA
Lexington, KY
17 September 2019